VEILED DECEPTION

BY
JERZY KROKOWSKI

About the Author

An emerging author who has recently published his debut novel, "Veiled Deception." Originally from Poland, Jerzy has found a home in the vibrant literary scene of Las Vegas, NV. His writing skills have gained recognition for their captivating and imaginative storytelling, unique perspective, and literary voice.

Published in USA, Las Vegas, NV. 2023
Cover design: LV SHOWS LIVE LLC
Text design: LV SHOWS LIVE LLC
First Edition

booksJK.com

To my Grandmother, Hanna

PROLOGUE

Control and manipulation can be achieved by using false hope and deception, leading those unsuspecting into a dismal and hopeless situation with a future of nothing but shattered dreams and broken promises.

Rage or love? On the one hand, love can drive people to do extraordinary things, but on the other, it can also become a fixation, an entanglement of lies and deceit that affects all involved.

In this story, you can find a group of people, who become connected in a perplexing and intricate knot of secrets and lies, and they need to confront their demons and accept the aftermath of their choices.

Motives, predominantly when driven by love, crime, and manipulation, can often be shrouded in ambiguity, making it challenging to discern the true intentions behind an individual's actions.

Explore the complicated world of false hope. Dear reader, come along with us as we explore passion and betrayal, which can be deceptive, and the truth can be hazardous to uncover.

CHAPTER 1

The sun cast a warm golden glow over the quiet suburban street, basking on the immaculate lawns and quaint houses in a serene light. One place, in particular, stood out among its neighbors: a two-story, white colonial with a well-manicured yard and a charming white picket fence. The vibrant flowers that adorned the garden seemed to dance in the gentle breeze, welcoming passersby with their sweet aroma. This idyllic abode was the home of Gary and Annie, a married couple who, from the outside, appeared to have achieved the American dream.

"Gary, are you almost ready?" Annie called out from the bottom of the staircase, her delicate hands gripping the railing as she peered up into the darkness above. Her voice quivered ever so slightly, betraying a mixture of anticipation and anxiety. As an artist who worked from home, Annie found solace in her creative endeavors, expressing herself with each stroke of the paintbrush on canvas. She often needed to catch up on time when immersed in her work but always set aside time to tend to the house and maintain its pristine appearance.

"Give me a minute. I'm wrapping up a call!" Gary's booming voice echoed down the stairs. A successful business executive, he worked long hours and was rarely home. The sound of his polished leather shoes clicking against the wooden floor signaled his approach, and Annie could feel her heart rate quicken. The surrounding air seemed to change, growing heavy with unspoken tension.

"All right, let's go," Gary said curtly, his piercing blue eyes locking onto Annie's for a moment before shifting away. Clad in a crisp, tailored suit, he exuded an aura of power and control. He held open the front door, waiting impatiently for Annie to slip past him before following her outside and locking the door behind them.

As they walked along the path, Annie couldn't help but steal a glance at her husband, taking in the strong lines of his jaw and the way his dark hair glistened under the sun. He had always been so handsome, and this charm had ensnared her all those years ago.

"Annie, keep up," Gary chided, not even bothering to look back at her as he strode ahead, his long legs effortlessly covering the ground. Annie hurried to catch up, suppressing the urge to reach out and take his hand. She knew better than to initiate any public displays of affection; they were reserved for the rare moments Gary felt inclined to be tender, which were few and far between.

As they continued, Annie's thoughts returned to her art studio, where her latest unfinished piece awaited her attention. Lately, she struggled to find inspiration, weighed down by the pressures of maintaining the perfect exterior of their home and the emotional turmoil that brewed beneath the surface. The creative spark that had once burned so brightly within her now seemed to flicker and wane, threatening to extinguish altogether.

"Annie, what's the matter?" Gary asked, finally turning to look at her. His voice was laced with annoyance, but Annie clung to the fact that he'd bothered to ask.

"Nothing, I'm fine," she replied quietly, forcing a smile and quickening her pace. As they walked side by side, the white colonial house with its immaculate lawn and picket fence receded into the distance, leaving behind a haunting reminder of the darkness lurking just beneath the surface of the perfect facade.

The morning sun glinted off the wet grass, casting a golden glow over the front yard. The white picket fence contrasted sharply with the vibrant array of flowers that adorned the neat flower beds, their petals unfurling in full bloom to greet the new day. Birds sang merrily from the branches of the ancient oak tree that stood sentinel over the two-story colonial house, its pristine white walls basking in the warmth of the sun's embrace. To any passerby, it was the picture-perfect embodiment of suburban bliss.

"Stand up straight, Annie," Gary hissed under his breath as they stood on the front porch, his fingers tightening around her arm like a vise. "And for God's sake, smile."

Annie flinched at the sharpness of his words but obediently complied, pasting a smile on her face that didn't quite reach her eyes. It was a dance they had performed countless times before, one where she tried desperately to avoid treading on his toes and stumbling into the abyss of his wrath.

"Did I not tell you to get rid of those weeds?" Gary continued, gesturing towards a tiny patch of dandelions that dared to mar the otherwise immaculate landscape of their garden. His voice was low and dangerous, a storm brewing beneath the calm facade.

"Yes, Gary, I'm sorry," Annie murmured, her gaze dropping to the ground, careful not to defy him by meeting his eyes. She knew all too well the consequences of stepping out of line. Over the years, Gary's cruelty had escalated from harsh words and belittlement to physical violence that left her body bruised and battered.

"Sorry isn't good enough, Annie." Gary's grip tightened, causing her to wince in pain. "I expect perfection from you. We can't have the neighbors thinking we're anything less than perfect, can we?"

"Of course not, Gary," she replied, her voice barely audible. Her heart pounded as she mentally prepared herself for the blow that was surely coming.

"Good." Gary's lips curled into a cruel smile. "Now fix it, and don't let me catch you slacking again."

As he released her arm and strode back into the house, Annie massaged the red imprint that his fingers had left on her skin. She swallowed the lump of fear that lodged in her throat like a stone, steeling herself against the reality of her life behind the closed doors of their seemingly perfect home.

The outside world saw a successful businessman and his talented artist wife living in harmony within their suburban paradise. They didn't see the shattered woman who fought to maintain the illusion of happiness, who bore the weight of her husband's anger and resentment like an albatross around her neck. They didn't see the tears that stained her pillow each night or the bruises that bloomed beneath her clothes like a macabre tapestry. And so, the cycle continued, the gulf between appearance and reality widening with each passing day.

The late afternoon sun cast long shadows across the lawns of the quiet suburban neighborhood. A group of women gathered on the porch of Mrs. Thompson's home, sipping iced tea and exchanging idle gossip. Within earshot, they could hear the distant laughter of children playing in a nearby yard. The air was thick with a sense of community, of shared lives and experiences that bound them together like invisible threads.

"Did you see Annie this morning?" whispered Mrs. Thompson, her eyes darting towards the white colonial house down the street. "She had long sleeves on again. In this heat! You'd think she'd have more sense."

"Maybe she's trying to cover up something," said another woman, her voice heavy with insinuation. "You know how Gary can be."

The other women exchanged knowing glances, their silence a tacit acknowledgment of the dark secret that lurked behind the pristine facade of Gary and Annie's home. They all knew about the abuse, but none of them wanted to be the one to break the unspoken code of silence that governed their small town. It was easier to look the other way and pretend not to notice the bruises peeking from beneath Annie's carefully chosen clothes.

"Someone should say something," murmured Mrs. Evans, shifting uncomfortably in her seat. "It's just not right."

"Mind your own business," chided Mrs. Thompson. "We've all got our crosses to bear."

Meanwhile, inside the white colonial house, the reality was far from the picture-perfect image it projected. The door swung open, revealing a cluttered hallway filled with discarded shoes, piles of mail, and an overturned vase that Gary had knocked over in a fit of rage days earlier. He hadn't bothered to clean it up, insisting it was Annie's responsibility.

"Annie!" Gary barked, slamming the door shut behind him. "I told you to clean up this mess."

Annie emerged from the kitchen, her hands still damp from washing dishes. The sink was piled high with dirty plates and glasses, a testament to Gary's neglect of even the most basic household chores. He claimed such tasks were beneath him, that his time was too valuable to be wasted on menial labor.

"Sorry, Gary," Annie said softly, careful not to meet his gaze. "I'll get to it right away."

"See what you do," he growled, stalking off toward the living room. As he disappeared from view, she allowed herself a moment of defiance, clenching her fists and silently cursing the man who had made her life a living hell.

"I can't do this anymore," she thought, her heart heavy with despair. "There has to be a way out."

But for now, she knew that there was no escape. She was trapped in a gilded cage, her every move watched and controlled by the man she had once loved. She stands next to the sink, trying to organize the mess unsuccessfully, but after a few plates, she gives up and, with wetted eyes, starts staring through the window.

Her thoughts were going wild. Daydreaming about the time she can be free from her life. And outside their home, the neighbors continued their quiet lives, unwilling or unable to intervene.

The next morning sun cast a warm, golden glow across the fence. Annie stood in the garden, her gloved hands gently cradling the fragile petals of a rose as she inspected it for signs of disease or pests. She dedicated hours to tending each flower daily, pruning and nourishing them with an almost maternal devotion. The vibrant blooms were her sanctuary, her escape from the chaos that lurked behind closed doors. And the impeccable front yard was her shield, a carefully constructed facade meant to convince the world that everything was perfect within their suburban haven.

"Annie, are you still in the garden?" Gary's voice cut through the tranquil silence, shattering her reverie.

"Coming," she replied, her pulse quickening at his footsteps approaching. She quickly removed her gloves and grabbed her gardening tools, dreading the confrontation that awaited her inside. As she turned to face her husband, she forced herself to smile despite the fear that gripped her heart.

"Enough with the gardening, Annie," he said dismissively, his eyes narrowing as they scanned the lush landscape. "You've spent enough time out there."

"I'm just trying to keep the yard looking nice," she murmured, her gaze fixed on the ground to avoid meeting his contemptuous stare. She could feel his eyes lingering on the long sleeves and pants that concealed the bruises he had inflicted upon her the night before.

"Nice? Is that what you call this?" he scoffed, gesturing towards the perfectly trimmed hedges and the rows of colorful flowers that danced in the gentle breeze. "It's a pathetic attempt to hide your shame. Make breakfast."

"Gary, please," she whispered, her chest tightening as she struggled to maintain her composure. "I just want to make sure our home looks presentable."

"Presentable?" he barked, his face contorting with rage. "You want to make it look like you have everything under control. You think that if our house looks perfect on the outside, no one will suspect what a failure you are on the inside, piece of the trash you are..."

"Please, let's not do this out here," she begged, acutely aware of their neighbors' watchful eyes peeking through parted curtains and over well-trimmed hedges.

"Fine," he spat, grabbing her arm roughly and pulling her towards the house. "Let's go discuss your failures in private."

Annie winced as she felt the pressure of his grip on her bruised flesh, but she knew better than to protest. Instead, she focused on the rhythmic sound of their footsteps on the gravel path, allowing it to anchor her to the present moment. And as they crossed the threshold into their home's messy, cluttered interior, she closed her eyes. She imagined herself in her garden, surrounded by the beauty and tranquility she desperately craved.

The morning light filtered through the curtains, casting a shadow across the room. Gary stood by the window, sipping his coffee as he peered out into the neighborhood. Annie sat at the kitchen table, nervously picking at her toast. Although they were just a few feet apart, their silence felt like miles.

"Annie," Gary said without turning to face her. "Don't forget we have that dinner party at the Thompsons' tonight."

"Of course not," she replied, her voice barely above a whisper. She knew it was essential to keep up appearances and attend social events with their neighbors. But the thought of spending another evening pretending everything was fine made her stomach churn.

"Make sure you wear something nice," he added, glancing in her direction. "And put on some makeup. You look like garbage."

His words stung, but she nodded obediently. She would find a way to hide the marks he'd left on her body, just as she had done countless times before.

Later that day, after Gary had left for work, Annie retreated to her art studio. The small room was filled with canvases, brushes, and paints – a chaotic jumble of colors and textures mirrored her inner turmoil. Once a sanctuary where she could lose herself in her work, the space now seemed foreign and unwelcoming.

She stared at a half-finished painting, hoping to find some semblance of inspiration. But all she could see were the shadows that haunted her daily life: the contorted faces of anger and fear, the dark corners where secrets festered. Her once vibrant creations had become muted and somber, reflecting the pain that consumed her.

Annie picked up a brush, her hands trembling as she tried to bring life to the canvas. But the strokes were hesitant and disjointed, echoing her fragmented thoughts. Exhaustion weighed heavily on her shoulders, making it impossible to focus. Finally, she dropped the brush; her body slumped in defeat.

"Annie, what's wrong with you?" she muttered, fighting back tears. "Why can't you just paint like you used to?"

But she knew the answer all too well. The abuse had left her drained, both physically and emotionally. It had stolen her passion, confidence, and even her sense of self. And as much as she longed to reclaim her art, she couldn't escape the suffocating grip of her reality.

As the hours ticked by, Annie tried to shake off her despair and prepare for the evening ahead. She chose a modest dress that covered the bruises on her arms and legs, applying makeup to conceal any lingering traces of pain. But as she looked in the mirror, she couldn't help but feel like a stranger – an imposter wearing a mask of happiness.

"Gary and Annie," she thought bitterly, "the perfect couple."

As Annie stood in the kitchen, her heart raced with each passing minute. The ticking of the clock on the wall seemed to grow louder and louder, drilling into her skull like a relentless metronome. Her breathing became shallow, and she clutched the counter's edge for support, fighting back waves of nausea. It was as if the walls were closing around her, trapping her in a prison of her own.

"Annie, you need to calm down," she whispered to herself, attempting to steady her nerves with a shaky breath. "You know what happens when Gary sees you like this."

Outside, storm clouds gathered overhead, casting dark shadows across the once-pristine lawn. The wind picked up, rattling the windows and causing the old oak tree's branches to sway ominously. It seemed as though even nature was conspiring against her, adding to the oppressive darkness that had consumed her life.

"Have you seen my tie?" Gary's voice boomed from upstairs, shattering her momentary reprieve.

"Which one, dear?" she called back, struggling to keep her voice steady. "The blue or the red?"

"Does it matter? Just bring them both!" he snapped, his temper flaring at the slightest provocation.

Annie hurried to retrieve the ties, her hands trembling as she held them out to her husband. Their eyes met for a brief second – a fleeting glimpse of the terror that lay beneath the surface of their strained relationship.

"Yeah," Gary muttered, snatching the ties from her grasp and turning away without another word.

As Annie retreated to the relative safety of the kitchen, her thoughts began to spiral out of control. The anxiety and depression that had plagued her for years threatened to consume her completely, leaving her feeling more trapped than ever before.

"Is this really my life?" she thought despairingly, tears welling up in her eyes. "How did I end up here, a prisoner in my home?"

Shattering glass startled her from her thoughts, followed by Gary's enraged roar. Her heart pounded in her chest as she realized his anger was escalating – becoming more unpredictable and dangerous each day.

"Annie, get in here and clean this mess up!" he bellowed, his voice shaking the very foundations of their crumbling façade.

"Coming, Gary," she choked out, wiping away her tears and steeling herself for what lay ahead.

As she entered the living room, she couldn't help but notice how the shards of glass on the floor seemed to mirror the shattered pieces of her spirit – broken and shattered beyond repair. And as she knelt to clean up the remnants of Gary's rage, she couldn't shake the chilling sense of foreboding that had settled over her like a dark cloud.

"Please, let this storm pass," she prayed silently, fearing not only for her own life but also for the lives of those who might become entangled in the destructive path of her husband's wrath.

CHAPTER 2

The rusty U-Haul truck rattled down Maple Street, stopping in front of the quaint blue house with white shutters. Sebastian stepped out of the driver's seat and surveyed his new neighborhood. The lawns were freshly mown, the smell of grass lingering in his nose, tickling his senses. The grass was perfectly cut, and the houses were a sea of pastel colors beneath the azure sky. Everything about it screamed suburban bliss.

Everything except the house next door.

The house was a different story. Its walls were painted a fainted white, and its windows were only partially open as if the occupants were trying to keep something inside or out. The shutters were closed tight, obscuring whatever lay within, and the whole place felt oppressive stillness that made Sebastian uneasy.

He turned away from the house, heading towards his new home, when he heard a voice behind him.

"Welcome to the neighborhood,"

Sebastian turned to face the owner of the voice and looked at a beautiful woman, her long black hair cascading down her shoulders and a sultry grin spreading across her face. She was dressed in a tight-fitting black dress that left little to the imagination, and her high heels clicked against the pavement with each step she took toward him.

Sebastian felt a chill run down his spine as he took in the woman's beauty and the ominous feeling that emanated from the house next door. He was about to respond when he felt her hand lightly brush against his own.

"I'm Amara," she purred, her voice seductive.

Sebastian swallowed hard, feeling a mix of desire and fear. He knew he should ignore her advances and focus on unpacking, but he found it hard to resist her charms.

Amara leaned in closer, sensing his hesitation, her body pressing against his. "I think you and I could have some fun. Sebastian took a step back, almost losing the balance. "Eee, no, thank you." He still couldn't take his eyes off her, but eventually, turning away, he grabbed the bag from the sidewalk and moved towards the door.

"I only live a few houses away if you ever need me, sexy." Sebastian didn't even turn away from the door. "That's not why I'm here," he mumbled, but his thought was already undressing Amara right there on the middle of the sidewalk. He knew that if he turned his head around, it would be tough to resist the temptation of the beautiful woman. Sebastian walked into his new house and started taking curtains from the window. His attention caught the next-door house. Through the bay window, Sebastian spotted a woman huddled in the corner of the living room, her husband looming over her. Even from a distance, Sebastian could see the rage burning in the man's eyes as he spits angry words at the cowering woman.

Sebastian's hands curled into fists, rage boiling in his gut. He knew abuse when he saw it. His childhood had been filled with similar scenes; his mother cowed under the iron fist of his drunken father. As a child, he swore that he would save people like his mother. And now, it seemed, he had found his first rescue.

The man - Gary, Sebastian recalled from the welcome packet - stormed out of the house, slamming the door behind him. Sebastian watched with hawk eyes as Gary climbed into his BMW and screeched out of the driveway.

Once Gary was out of sight, Sebastian approached the house next door, his heart pounding. He rang the bell and waited. After a long moment, the door creaked open.

Annie stood there, and her eyes rimmed red. Bruises mottled her pale arms. But despite it all, she was striking - wisps of blonde hair framing her heart-shaped face, full lips, and eyes the color of the summer sky.

"I'm Sebastian," he said gently. "I'm your new neighbor. I couldn't help but notice that you seem to be in some distress. I wanted to make sure you were all right."

Annie stared at him, a mix of fear, hope, and suspicion in her gaze. Sebastian kept his expression open, projecting only concern and compassion. Suddenly Annie looked into his eyes, and he thought he saw a smile in the corner of the cut lip. But then Sebastian composed himself and thought, "How can that be? Did I see that, or it's just my imagination?"

Finally, Annie stepped back and opened the door wider. "Please, come in."

Sebastian smiled, stepping over the threshold. His plan was working perfectly. Soon, he would have Annie right where he wanted her - safe in his arms, far away from the abuse and pain of her sad excuse for a husband.

All he needed was time. With time, he could gain her trust. With trust, he could save her.

And once he saved her, she would be his forever.

Sebastian watched Gary enter the car and drive to work the next day. He picked up the basket, unpacked the delivery, picked a few fruits and vegetables, placed them into the basket, and a moment later, he was standing on the porch of Annie's house. "I had a bumper crop of tomatoes and cucumbers this year. I thought I'd share."

Annie's eyes lit up. "Thank you, that's so kind."

"Not at all," Sebastian said. "I'm happy to help in any way I can. After all, what are neighbors for?". Then he spotted that one of the apples had a sticker from the store. Sebastian swiftly grabbed the apple, jiggled it in his hands for a second, scratched the label, and handed it to Annie. "Hope you like the red ones?"

He spent the afternoon with Annie, discussing books they both enjoyed, from classic literature to mystery novels. Annie seemed starved for conversation and company. Sebastian made a mental note to isolate her from outside social connections. It would make her more dependent on him.

As Sebastian made his way from the hallway into the living room, he surveyed the scene before him. Old, faded floral couches littered the room, the television flickering silently in the background. Stray toys were scattered across the carpeted floor, remnants of happier times in the house before Gary.

Annie sat on one of the couches, motioning for Sebastian to take the other one. He sat down beside her, keeping a considerable distance between them not to scare her off. "Can I get you anything?" he asked.

"No," she whispered, staring down at her lap. "Thank you for coming over, Sebastian. I don't know what's happening to me."

Sebastian's heart ached as he looked at her, the bruises on her arms like dark accusations against her husband. "You don't have to put up with this, Annie. You deserve better. I know you do."

Annie looked up at him then, her tears glistening in the light. "I know," she whispered. "But I don't know how to leave."

Sebastian took her hand, feeling the tremble of her fingers. "I can help you," he said, his voice firm and sure. "I'll help you leave and find a safe place. You don't have to be afraid anymore."

Annie's eyes met his, and he saw a moment of trust and hope in them. Sebastian felt a thrill of excitement. This was it. This was the moment he had been waiting for. He would be her savior, her hero.

But even as he smiled down at her, Sebastian couldn't help but wonder what would happen once he had her away from Gary. Would she indeed be his? Would she love him the way he loved her?

For now, he pushed those thoughts aside and focused on the task. He would save Annie, no matter what it took. And then, only then, could they indeed be together.

Sebastian spent the rest of the evening with Annie, devising a plan to get her out of the house and away from Gary. He could see the fear in her eyes and a glimmer of hope as they talked. He hoped that she could finally be free from the abuse and control of her husband.

Sebastian felt a sense of satisfaction as he left her house that night. He was doing something good. He was making a difference in someone's life. And he couldn't wait to see the look on Annie's face when he finally saved her.

But even as he walked back to his own house, Sebastian couldn't shake the doubts in his mind. Was he really doing the right thing? Was he genuinely helping Annie or manipulating her for his own gain?

He pushed those thoughts aside, reminding himself of his noble intentions. He was doing this for Annie. For her safety and happiness. And he had another big reason.

Leaving the house, Sebastian placed a hidden camera in the bushes, angled to capture the kitchen and living room. He wanted to keep an eye on Gary and how he behaved when Sebastian wasn't around.

That evening, he reviewed the footage, rage building inside as he witnessed Gary berating and grabbing Annie roughly. His fists clenched, longing to punish the pathetic bully.

No. He had to remain patient for Annie's sake.

The next day, he invited Annie over for dinner, serving her homemade lasagna, her favorite. As she ate with enthusiasm, he watched her with a mix of affection and hunger. Soon, he thought, she would be his. And he would treasure her always, keeping her safe in a gilded cage, away from the harshness and cruelty of the outside world.

After dinner, he rechecked the cameras. He had to know Gary's routines and his weaknesses. The time would come when he would make his move.

And Gary would never see it coming.

Sebastian and Annie spent much time together for the next few weeks. She slowly opened up to him while he talked to her about his plans to take her away from Gary. She even revealed the times when Gary was at his worse, describing in detail what it was like living with him.

Sebastian felt a blazing anger inside himself whenever he heard these stories, and he wanted nothing more than to protect her from this man and his cruelty once and for all.

One cold evening, as they sat in front of the fire in Sebastian's house talking about her past, Annie began to cry softly. He put an arm around her shoulder and held her close, whispering soothing words until she calmed down.

The heat between them was undeniable; as they looked into each other's eyes, they both knew that something had changed between them that night. It wasn't just about saving Annie anymore; it had become something else entirely.

Two weeks later, the sun filtered through Annie's curtains one morning as Sebastian helped her pack a small suitcase. His heart raced with equal parts excitement and anxiety. Today was the day.

"Are you sure about this?" Annie asked, her hands trembling. "What if he finds us?"

Sebastian grasped her hands firmly. "I won't let that happen. You can trust me."

He saw the flicker of doubt in her eyes and felt a pang. Did she not realize he only wanted to protect her?

After packing the essentials, he called Gary's cell phone from a burner phone, disguising his voice. "Mr. Miller? This is Officer Smith. There's been an accident at your worksite. Please come immediately."

As Gary sputtered his confused reply, Sebastian ended the call with a smirk. That would get rid of him for at least a couple of hours.

"It's time," he said gently to Annie.

They crept out the back door and hurried to his car. Suddenly he said, "Let's come to my place first. I need to grab some things."

He had done it. He had saved her.

"Stay here, pushing her into the home. I need to do one more thing." Hey grabbed the notepad, wrote a note, and ran to Annie's house. Walk back through the back door and drop the message on the table: "I have enough. I'm leaving you forever. Don't look for me. I'm leaving the state - Annie".

Sebastian quickly searched the drawers in the kitchen and grabbed the ring and wedding band Annies' had left on the table. "That can't be wasted. She will wear that for me," he mumbled under his nose and disappeared in the back door again.

He walked to his house, Annie went silent, and he felt her tension easing in his arms. She was still anxious but would accept her new circumstances in time.

He led her downstairs to the basement. It was furnished but very cluttered and dirty, like none was here for a decade. The room has a bed, bathroom, and laundry sink. Annie stared at him, eyes wide and hollow. He kissed her forehead, brushing aside her hair. "Don't worry. I'll keep you safe. You'll be comfortable here," he said. "I'll bring you meals and anything else you need. But this is where you'll stay when I have to leave the house."

"Leave the house?" Her voice rose in panic. "You're locking me in?"

He cupped her face gently. "It's for your own safety, my love. Gary will be looking for you. He can't find you here."

"No, please..." She struggled against him as he guided her into the room.

"Shh. It's all right." He wrapped his arms around her, pinning her arms to her sides. "You'll see. This is for the best. I'll take good care of you, Annie. You're mine now...and you'll never escape".

When Sebastian left the basement and heard the lock turning on the door, she knew... this was not what she expected from the rescue. She panicked and started deep breathing, "I can't stay here," she said, but it was too late...

Sebastian slept well that night. The trap had been sprung. There was no escape now. Annie was his.

CHAPTER 3

The rain fell in a relentless drizzle, the droplets pooling together on the slick pavement of the town's only police station. Gary stood outside, his eyes shifting nervously, his hands clenched into fists. He could feel the anger boiling beneath his skin, a familiar sensation that had accompanied him for as long as he could remember. The air tasted metallic, and the dampness seeped into his very bones. The station's neon sign flickered erratically, casting ominous shadows on the ground.

"Detective Olivia!" Gary barked, his voice cutting through the downpour as he barged into the station, water dripping from his wet hair. "I need to report my wife missing!"

The detective looked up from her paperwork, her eyes narrowing at the sight of Gary. She was a tall woman with a strong jawline and expressive eyes that held an unwavering determination. Her gaze bore into him like a hawk's, assessing and calculating.

"Annie's been gone for three days," Gary continued, his chest heaving with frustration. "I can't find her anywhere."

"Mr. Miller," Detective Olivia said coolly, pushing her chair back and standing up. "We're aware of the situation between you and your wife. Are you sure she didn't leave because she wanted to?"

Gary bristled at the insinuation, anger flaring within him. His eyes narrowed, and he fought the urge to lash out. Even here, surrounded by the town's police force, his abusive nature threatened to rise to the surface. He couldn't help it; it was a part of him, a sickening thread woven into the fabric of his being.

"Of course not!" he snapped. "She's in danger, I know it. You have to help me find her. I found the note, but it's not her handwriting."

Detective Olivia folded her arms across her chest, her stance rigid. She exchanged a glance with another officer, who shook his head ever so slightly. It was clear to Gary that they weren't willing to help him.

"Mr. Miller," Detective Olivia said, her voice devoid of sympathy. "The entire town knows about your... issues with your wife. We're unsure if we can trust your judgment on this matter."

"Are you kidding me?" Gary's voice cracked with desperation. "My wife is missing, and you're going to let that crap get in the way of helping her?"

"Gary," the detective replied, her tone firm. "I understand that you're concerned. But given your history, we have to consider all possibilities. I'll look into it, but I can't promise anything now."

The weight of the town's apathy towards Annie's suffering hung heavy in the air, suffocating Gary as he stood there, his hands shaking with anger and fear. He knew that his actions had led to this moment, but he couldn't accept the consequences. He needed to find Annie and would do whatever it took to make that happen.

"Fine," he spat, turning on his heel and storming out of the station. As the door slammed behind him, the rain continued to pour down, a fitting reflection of the storm brewing within his tormented soul.

Gary walked the town streets, his frustration simmering as he saw the townspeople huddled under awnings and in doorways, whispering and casting furtive glances at him. He knew their gossip was poison, a slow-acting venom that would erode any chance he had of finding Annie with the community's help. The rain continued to fall, and each icy drop echoed his desperation.

"Have you seen her?" Gary asked a group of women who stood outside the local grocery store, clutching their shopping bags close to their chests. Their eyes darted from side to side, avoiding his gaze.

"Sorry, Mr. Miller, we haven't seen anything," one of the women replied, her voice trembling slightly. "And we don't want to get involved."

"Involved? My wife is missing!" Gary snapped, his anger flaring. "How can you just stand there and do nothing?"

"Gary, please," another woman said, her eyes downcast. "We've got our own families to worry about."

"Fine!" Gary spat, stalking away from them. He felt a bitter rage rising within him, fueled by the fear of what might have happened to Annie. How could these people who had once been his friends now turn their backs on him? On Annie?

As he wandered through the town, he began to piece together fragments of truth, scraps of information concealed beneath layers of avoidance and secrecy. He found himself growing more and more desperate, willing to take any risk, make any sacrifice to uncover the truth, and find his missing wife.

"Annie..." Gary muttered, his voice barely audible above the sound of the rain. "Where are you?"

Gary walked along the town's main street, his steps weighed down by the burden of his search and the whispers that trailed behind him like shadows. The once-familiar storefronts now seemed cold and unwelcoming, their windows reflecting the distorted image of a man he hardly recognized.

"Can you believe it?" he overheard a woman say to her friend as they passed, not bothering to lower their voices. "Annie's been gone for weeks, and no one seems to care. Not even the police."

"Maybe they know something we don't," the other replied with a conspiratorial glance in Gary's direction. "You know what they say about the husband always being the first suspect."

"Shh! He'll hear you," the first woman hissed, but Gary had already heard enough.

"Excuse me," he interrupted his voice tight with barely-contained anger. "I'm doing everything I can to find my wife. If you have any useful information or suggestions, I'd be more than happy to listen. Otherwise, keep your face shut!"

The women stared at him, their eyes wide with shock and fear. They muttered hasty apologies before hurrying away, leaving Gary alone once more.

"Are you okay?" Mrs. Thompson, the elderly neighbor, appeared beside him, looking up at him with concern etched into the lines of her face. "I couldn't help but overhear…"

"Doesn't anyone around here have anything better to do than spread rumors?" Gary snapped, the frustration bubbling over inside him. "My wife is missing, and all this town cares about is idle gossip!"

"Gary," Mrs. Thompson said softly, gently touching his arm. "Not everyone believes those rumors. Some of us want to see Annie found just as much as you do."

"Then why isn't anyone doing anything to help? Why am I the only one searching?" The anguish in his voice was palpable, and for a moment, Mrs. Thompson seemed at a loss for words.

"Perhaps," she said, her eyes filled with sadness, "it's because we're all afraid of what might be found."

Gary stared at her, his mind racing as he tried to decipher the meaning behind her words. As if sensing his confusion, Mrs. Thompson sighed, her gaze distant.

"Sometimes, Gary, it's easier to believe the worst than to confront the truth. People like a simple answer – even if it means sacrificing someone else's happiness or reputation."

Her words echoed in his ears, a haunting reminder of his actions' consequences upon himself, Annie, and the town they called home. And as he walked away, leaving Mrs. Thompson alone on the sidewalk, he couldn't shake the feeling that the solution to his wife's disappearance was hidden somewhere in the shadows that surrounded them both.

A sudden gust of wind tore through the street, sending a shiver down Gary's spine. He pulled his coat tighter around him, his thoughts swirling like the leaves dancing around him.

"Annie," he whispered, barely audible above the howling wind. "Where are you?"

And as the first drops of rain began to fall, soaking into the fabric of his clothes and chilling him to the bone, Gary felt a sudden sense of dread wash over him. It was as if the universe itself were trying to warn him that, no matter how hard he searched or how desperately he fought against the darkness, no easy answers would be waiting for him at the end of this journey.

For the truth, he realized with sinking despair, was far more complex and twisted than anything he could ever have imagined – and the path that lay before him was one from which there could be no turning back.

"I'm sure he killed her," said Mrs. Thompson, "we just need to find her body."

Gary froze, the words ringing in his ears like an accusatory bell tolling the end of his hope. He turned to face her, his heart pounding in his chest.

"What? What did you say?" His voice was barely above a whisper.

"I'm sorry, dear," Mrs. Thompson said, her eyes filled with sorrow. "But I can't ignore the signs any longer. Something terrible must have happened to Annie, and I'm afraid your actions may have led her to a tragic end."

Gary staggered back, his mind reeling with shock and disbelief. He had never expected to hear such accusations from someone he had once trusted as a friend.

"You don't know what you're talking about," he said, his voice shaking with emotion. "I would never hurt Annie. I loved her."

"Love can be a strange and dangerous force," Mrs. Thompson said softly.

CHAPTER 4

Detective Olivia stood in the center of the bustling station, her eyes scanning the room as she took in the chaos surrounding her. The air was thick with tension and the scent of stale coffee, which mingled with the palpable fear that had settled over the town since Annie's disappearance. It clung to the walls and seeped into every corner like an all-consuming fog. Despite the case's urgency, Olivia couldn't help but feel a deep sense of satisfaction at being in the heart of it all. Her fingers twitched with anticipation as she clenched her notepad tightly, eager to bring justice to light.

"All right, everyone, listen up!" Olivia called out, her voice ringing loud and clear above the cacophony of voices. The room fell silent, and all eyes turned to her, waiting for instructions. She took a deep breath, knowing that the weight of this case rested on her shoulders. "We're going to find Annie, but we must do this by the book. That means no cutting corners and no jumping to conclusions."

As she spoke, she could see the faces around her nodding in agreement, but there was one face she couldn't quite read - Gary's. The man who once controlled Annie with an iron fist now looked lost, his eyes empty and hollow. Olivia knew that involving him in the investigation was risky, but she also knew that he might be the key to finding Annie.

"Gary," she said firmly, looking him in the eye. "You need to understand that you're not in charge here. We have to work together to find Annie, which means putting your personal feelings aside."

He nodded slowly, but Olivia could see the resentment simmering beneath the surface. She knew that she would have to keep a close eye on him, but for now, she had more significant problems to deal with.

As the police team began to disperse, Olivia felt a tap on her shoulder. She turned to find the concerned face of one of her officers, Martha. "Detective," she whispered urgently, "the townspeople are starting to get suspicious of everyone, especially Sebastian. They're demanding that we investigate him more thoroughly, but some of them seem reluctant to help."

"Sebastian?" Olivia asked, her brow furrowing in thought. The enigmatic newcomer had caught her attention from the moment he arrived in town, and she couldn't shake the feeling that there was more to him than met the eye. He had shown an unusual interest in Annie, which only fueled the people's suspicions.

"Why Sebastian? He just came into the town. Do you think that he's involved?" - Olivia asked. "Do you really believe in everything you hear from the people in this town?"

"No." Martha spread her arms, and Olivia thought for a split second that she looked like the angel that would take off the ground just in a moment. "No, I don't believe in everything," Martha continues, "But if you hear from the closes neighbors that they have seen him quite often in recent weeks around the house, then I think we should check that. Remember? - Follow the evidence..."

"Yeah, yeah... All right," said Olivia, her voice filled with determination. "I want you to gather all the information you can on Sebastian. Talk to his neighbors, look into his background, and find out if he has any connection to Annie. But be discreet – we don't want to tip him off just yet."

"Understood, Detective," Martha replied before slipping away to carry out her orders.

As Olivia watched her go, she couldn't shake the feeling that they were missing something crucial, a piece of the puzzle that would bring everything into focus. She knew that the answers were hidden within the shadows of the town, and it was up to her to uncover them. But as the sun dipped below the horizon and street lights came on, she couldn't help but wonder who or what was lurking in those dark corners, waiting to strike.

The rain had set in, casting a dreary pallor over the small town. Rivulets of water snaked through the cracks in the pavement as Detective Olivia and her team trudged from door to door; the weight of the waterlogged air was heavy on their shoulders. It was as if the very heavens mourned Annie's disappearance, shedding tears that soaked into the earth like unspoken secrets.

"Mrs. Thompson? I'm Detective Olivia, and this is Officer Stevens," Olivia said as she stood on the doorstep of the kindly old woman who lived three doors down from Annie. "We're investigating Annie's disappearance and wondered if you might have seen anything unusual lately."

"Annie?" Mrs. Thompson repeated, her brow knitting with concern. She shook her head slowly, and her eyes clouded with confusion. "I'm afraid not, dear. I've been so busy with my garden club that I haven't had much time to chat with the neighbors. But I do hope you find her soon – poor girl."

"Thank you, Mrs. Thompson," Olivia replied, a polite smile gracing her lips as she left. She couldn't shake the unease that settled in her gut, gnawing at her resolve like a dog worrying a bone. The townspeople's reluctance to discuss Sebastian was troubling, and she couldn't help but wonder if they were harboring some dark secret that would lead her to the truth.

"Detective, are you all right?" Officer Jenkins asked, his brows furrowing with concern as he noticed the troubled expression on her face.

"Something's not adding up," Olivia muttered, her frustration mounting with each passing moment. The town's collective silence felt like a barrier, impeding her progress and obscuring the path leading her to Annie.

"Maybe we should try another approach," suggested Jenkins, his hand resting on her shoulder in a gesture of reassurance. "We could talk to Annie's friends or her coworkers. Someone has to know something."

"Right, just she works for herself," Olivia agreed, nodding with renewed determination. "Let's follow up on that friend's lead. The truth is out there – we have to uncover it."

As they continued their investigation, the townspeople's opinions seemed to split like the lightning that fractured the dark sky overhead. Some pointed fingers at Gary, unwilling to believe that someone else could be responsible for Annie's disappearance. Others whispered about Sebastian, casting sidelong glances in his direction as they huddled together, trading secrets like currency.

"Detective," called Martha, one of the officers who had been tasked with gathering information on Sebastian.

"I managed to speak with a few of his coworkers. They say he's a bit of a loner but never showed any signs of violent tendencies. However, I can't find any information about him past ten years."

"What do you mean? You can't find anything beyond ten years?" Olivia asked with a surprised tone. "He must come from somewhere. He must have some past beyond that. He wasn't born ten years ago. Please start digging into it."

"Of course, detective, I will, " said Marta, returning to her desk.

"Thank you, Martha," Olivia replied, her frustration threatening to spill over like the rainwater cascading from the gutters above. She gritted her teeth, determined not to let her emotions cloud her judgment. "Keep digging. We'll get to the bottom of this."

As the storm raged outside, Olivia felt a tempest brewing within her heart. She knew that time was running out, and with each passing moment, the chances of finding Annie alive grew slimmer. The town's division threatened to fracture the very foundations of their community, leaving them all vulnerable to the darkness that lurked just beneath the surface.

"Annie," she whispered into the wind, her voice barely audible over the howling gale. "Where are you?"

Meanwhile, in the damp, dimly lit basement of Sebastian's home, the air was thick with tension and unspoken truths. Annie sat on a cold concrete floor, her wrists bound behind her back and her eyes wide with a mixture of fear and determination. She studied the room, taking in every detail – the pipes that snaked along the ceiling, the dirt-caked windows that barely let in any light, and the heavy metal door that separated her from the world outside.

Sebastian paced back and forth, his dark hair framing a face that seemed engaged in an eternal struggle between deep concern and sinister intent. His gaze flickered to Annie every few moments before he would turn away as if unable to meet her eyes for long.

"Annie," he said, his voice low but filled with a hidden intensity. "Why did you have to do this? Why did you involve me?"

Annie's heart raced in her chest, but she refused to give Sebastian the satisfaction of seeing her squirm. Instead, she focused on the memories of her life with Gary – the countless nights of pain and terror she had endured and the twisted revenge fantasies that had played out in her mind like a silent film reel.

"Me? I didn't do anything. I didn't do anything for years. I was there suffering". Annie paused momentarily and thought of the terrors she had lived through daily for the last ten years. She took a deep breath and decided to speak again.

"Because I needed help," she replied, her voice steady and eerily calm. "And you were the perfect person to provide it."

Sebastian clenched his fists, his knuckles turning white with the force of his grip. He could feel the weight of his darker obsessions pressing down on him, threatening to swallow him whole. In another life, he might have been Annie's savior; instead, he found himself her captor.

"Annie," he whispered, his voice wavering. "I never meant for it to come to this. But you've left me no choice."

As he left the room, locking the door behind him, Annie's thoughts raced. She knew she needed to escape, and her mind began formulating a plan. She had been observant of the room and its layout, and her twisted mind spun webs of deception.

In the dead of night, when Sebastian's snores echoed through the house, Annie made her move. She freed her wrists from their bindings with an elegant twist and a sharp crack. Wincing at the pain, she crept toward the door, her heart pounding like a drumbeat in her ears.

Her hands trembled as she reached for the lock, but a sudden creak from above stopped her in her tracks just as she turned the key. Sebastian stood at the top of the stairs, his eyes wide with shock and betrayal.

"Annie," he breathed, his voice barely above a whisper. "What have you done?"

As the heavy footsteps thundered down the stairs, Annie knew that her attempt at freedom had failed. She braced herself for the consequences, her heart rich with the knowledge that she had only traded one prison for another.

Sebastian stared at the locked door, his furrowed brow betraying a mixture of anger and concern. He believed that by keeping Annie captive, he was protecting her from the world outside, from herself. In his mind, it was an act of love, justified by the twisted notion that he alone could save her. His heart thudded in his chest as he took a deep breath, steeling himself for what he had to do next.

"Annie," he began, his voice soft and steady, "I'm doing this for your good. You can't be trusted out there. Not yet."

"Sebastian, please," Annie pleaded, her eyes shimmering with unshed tears. "You don't understand. I need to get away from here. Let's leave that place together," but her words were cut off as Sebastian shook his head firmly, silencing her.

"Enough," he said, his voice firm. "We'll talk later." And with that, he turned and ascended the stairs, leaving Annie alone in the dimly lit basement.

The first light of dawn painted the sky in a muted orange hue as Detective Olivia stood outside the local diner, her breath misting in the chill morning air. Her fingers tightened around the steaming cup of coffee in her hands, seeking warmth and comfort from the bitter cold. As she sipped the dark liquid, she couldn't ignore the palpable tension that had settled over the town like a heavy blanket.

"Morning, Olivia," called out a familiar voice. It was Tom, the diner's owner, his face worn yet friendly as he wiped down the countertop with a rag. "Seems like half the town's been here already, talking about what's happening."

"Can't say I'm surprised," Olivia replied, forcing a tight smile. "People are scared, Tom. They want answers, and they want them now."

"Too right they do," he agreed, tossing the rag over his shoulder. "But not everyone's so sure it's that Sebastian fellow you're after. Some still think old Gary finally snapped and did something to Annie himself."

Olivia sighed, feeling the weight of the investigation pressing down on her shoulders. "Both men have a motive, but we can't rule out any possibilities until we find solid evidence."

"Speaking of which," Tom said, lowering his voice conspiratorially, "You didn't hear this from me, but I heard some folks talking about a fight Gary and Annie had at the bar last week. Might be worth looking into."

"Thanks, Tom," Olivia responded, her brow furrowing in thought. "We'll follow up on that lead."

As she left the diner, Olivia couldn't help but feel the unease that had settled among the townspeople. Conversations ceased as she passed by, eyes narrowing with suspicion and fear. It seemed the entire town had turned against itself, casting blame and doubt upon one another.

"Detective Olivia!" a voice called out from behind her. She turned to see Sarah, one of the younger townspeople, rushing towards her, her cheeks flushed with exertion.

"Sarah, what's going on?" Olivia asked, concern etching her features.

"Something's happened," Sarah gasped, her breath ragged. "You need to come quickly."

Olivia's heart raced as she followed Sarah through the winding streets, her mind racing with possibilities. What new development had occurred? Had they found Annie at last?

As they rounded the corner onto a previously quiet residential street, Olivia was met with a scene that made her blood run cold. A small crowd had gathered around a single-story house, its once pristine white paint now marred by a sinister message scrawled in bold, red letters:

"YOU'LL NEVER FIND HER"

Olivia's eyes widened in shock, the implications of the message chilling her to the core. The time they were, they seemed to stand still as the gravity of the situation settled upon her like an oppressive weight.

"Annie..." she whispered, her voice barely audible above the crowd's murmurs.

CHAPTER 5

The sun dipped below the horizon, casting long shadows across the quiet streets of the small town. Streetlights flickered to life, their orange glow illuminating the damp pavement. Sebastian's vintage car stood parked outside his shop, its chrome gleaming under the lamplight. The keys dangled from the ignition, a careless oversight that seemed out of character for this newcomer who had been so meticulous in his dealings with life.

Mrs. Thompson peered at Sebastian's car through her lace curtains, her brow furrowed. She had seen him leave it unlocked on more than one occasion, and it struck her as odd. A gust of wind rustled the leaves around her window, and she shivered. "There's something off about that man," she muttered to herself, though she couldn't quite put her finger on it.

Peter strode along the sidewalk, hands shoved into his pockets, lost in thought about his recent conversations with Gary. As he passed Sebastian's home, he noticed the door slightly ajar. Peter hesitated, wondering if he should say something, but decided against it. He continued walking but couldn't shake the nagging feeling that something wasn't right.

"Have you noticed anything... odd about Sebastian?" Lucy asked Mrs. Thompson and Peter as they sat in her cafe the following morning. The wind howled outside, rattling the windows and sending raindrops pelting against the glass.

"Odd?" Mrs. Thompson echoed, stirring her tea absentmindedly. "Well, I've seen him leave his car unlocked several times. And last night, his garage door was wide open."

"Really? That doesn't sound like him," Peter mused, sipping his coffee. "I mean, since he arrived here, all he's done is try to help people and make friends. But now that you mention it, I did see him lurking around Gary's house the other night when he should have been at home."

"Maybe we're just being paranoid," Lucy said, her eyes darting to the window as a flash of lightning illuminated the dark sky. "But it feels like something is going on beneath the surface that we're not seeing."

"Indeed," Mrs. Thompson agreed, her voice barely audible above the rain. "It's as if he's hiding something."

"Or someone," Peter added, his gaze shifting between the two women. "I can't shake the feeling that Sebastian's actions are somehow connected to Gary and Annie."

"Whatever it is," Lucy whispered, her eyes narrowing with determination, "we won't let him hurt anyone in this town."

As the storm raged outside, the three of them sat huddled together in the cozy cafe, their suspicions growing darker and more tangled by the minute. All the while, the enigmatic figure of Sebastian loomed large in their thoughts, his motives remaining as elusive as the shadows cast by the flickering streetlights. The wind howled like a beast outside, rattling the windows of the quaint little cafe. Mrs. Thompson stared into her steaming cup of tea, her delicate hands trembling as she cradled it. Her mind raced with the thoughts of Sebastian's recent actions and the suspicions they had aroused.

"Should we confront him?" Lucy asked, her voice quivering with uncertainty. Peter shook his head. His eyes fixed on a raindrop trickling down the windowpane.

"Maybe not," he said softly, glancing toward Mrs. Thompson and Lucy. "We don't have any concrete evidence, just our intuition. And confronting him might make matters worse."

Mrs. Thompson sighed, the weight of their suspicions bearing down on her. Her heart ached with conflict; she didn't want to believe that someone as charming and kind as Sebastian could be involved in something sinister. After all, he had always been there for them, offering help whenever needed. Besides, who could forget Gary's constant unpleasantness?

"Remember when Gary yelled at Annie in the bar last time?" Lucy whispered, her face contorted with disgust. "Sebastian was the one who stepped in and calmed the situation down. It's hard to imagine him doing anything harmful."

Peter nodded, recalling the incident. The memory of Sebastian's gentle smile as he diffused the tense confrontation made the idea of him being involved in whatever was going on with Gary even more challenging to digest.

"Even if our suspicions are valid," Mrs. Thompson began, her voice barely audible over the sound of the storm, "we should be careful how we proceed. We don't want to cause trouble or put anyone in danger." She looked around the dimly lit cafe, the golden glow of the lamps casting soft shadows on the worn wooden furniture.

"Perhaps," Peter suggested, "we could keep an eye on him for now. If we notice anything more suspicious, we can take action then. But until then..." He trailed off, his gaze drifting back to the rain-lashed window.

"Until then, we give him the benefit of the doubt," Mrs. Thompson finished for him, her eyes meeting his with a mixture of determination and unease.

The three friends sat silently as the storm outside mirrored the chaos brewing within their hearts. The image of Sebastian's warm smile was etched into their minds—his charm and kindness clashing against the dark cloud of suspicion that surrounded him.

And as they grappled with their conflicting emotions, the line between friend and foe became ever more blurred.

In the following days, Sebastian's presence in their lives seemed to be a balm to their troubled thoughts. The winds had blown away the clouds of doubt, leaving clear skies and sun-kissed mornings behind. Peter laughed heartily with Sebastian as they helped repair the fence behind Mrs. Thompson's house. Lucy watched from her window as Sebastian offered to carry groceries for an elderly neighbor, his smile genuine and contagious.

"Maybe we were just overreacting," Lucy mused, her finger tracing the condensation on her coffee cup as she sat with Peter and Mrs. Thompson in the cafe. "I mean, look at him. He's genuinely helping people."

"True," Peter agreed, his gaze lingering on Sebastian chatting with a group of children outside the cafe. "He doesn't seem like someone who would harm anyone."

"Appearances can be deceiving," Mrs. Thompson cautioned, but even her voice lacked conviction. "But it does seem we may have misjudged him. I still think Garry killed her and buried her somewhere nearby".

"Stop it!" Lucy shouted, bringing everyone's attention to the cafe. All heads turn to her with some confusion and curiosity". All conversations end, and a sharp, quiet pause blasts the room. You could hear Lucy breathing on the other side of the cafe. She quickly took the plate from the table and disappeared in the back.

Same time doors open, and Olivia walks into the cafe. She stopped at the door and thought, 'How bad does that place become through the years.' She looked around and spotted the group of locals, turned right to them, and strolled.

"Detective Olivia Anderson," she introduced herself, extending a firm handshake to the people. "I've been assigned to assist with the ongoing investigation into Annie's disappearance."

"Ah, welcome, Detective," Peter's voice shook slightly as he stood up and greeted her quietly. "I'm Peter, and these are my friends, Mrs. Thompson and Lucy." He gestured awkwardly to the two women sitting beside him.

"Nice to meet you," Detective Olivia replied, shaking their hands firmly yet gently. Her eyes seemed to appraise them, weighing their worth like precious stones on a jeweler's scale. "I understand you three were close to Annie. Any information or insights you have would be invaluable."

"Of course," Mrs. Thompson said, her voice steady but her heart pounding. "We're here to help in any way we can."

As they shared their knowledge of Annie's life and her relationship with Gary, they couldn't help but feel a mixture of relief and unease. Detective Olivia's presence brought new hope for answers but also stirred up the nagging doubts about Sebastian that they had tried so hard to dismiss.

Later the day, Detective Olivia stood outside the small police station, a steaming cup of bitter coffee in hand as she surveyed the narrow streets of the sleepy town. The late afternoon sun cast long shadows across the cobblestones, and a gentle breeze rustled the leaves of the ancient oak trees that lined the main thoroughfare. She frowned, her eyes narrowing as she mulled over the case before her.

"Sebastian," she muttered under her breath, taking a long sip of her coffee. "What are you hiding?"

Over the next few days, Detective Olivia threw herself into her investigation. She scoured security footage from local businesses, looking for any sign of Sebastian in places he shouldn't have been. Late nights were spent poring over stacks of documents, searching for any hint of a pattern in his activities or inconsistencies in his alibi.

One evening, as she sat hunched over her desk, a sudden gust of wind blew through the open window, scattering papers everywhere. As she scrambled to collect them, a particular photograph caught her eye – a grainy image of Sebastian entering a building on the outskirts of town. The timestamp on the photo didn't align with where he claimed to have been.

"Gotcha," Detective Olivia whispered, her heart racing as she studied the picture more closely.

She began to delve deeper, cross-referencing the new information with witness accounts. One by one, she interviewed those who had interacted with Sebastian, her keen instincts guiding her through each conversation. A sense of unease began to gnaw at her stomach as she listened to their stories, each person seemingly unaware of the potential danger lurking beneath his charming facade.

"Everyone's so eager to trust him," she thought, frustration mounting. "But there's something off about him. I can feel it."

As she dug further into Sebastian's past, a pattern started to emerge. In each location where he had lived, there had been a series of unexplained incidents – mysterious fires, missing persons, inexplicable accidents. And then - nothing past ten years. While the evidence was circumstantial at best, it was enough to raise the hairs on the back of her neck.

"Could he really be involved in all of this?" Detective Olivia pondered, her brow furrowed as she stared into the dimly lit distance from her office window. The streetlights below cast an eerie orange glow, and the wind picked up once more, howling through the narrow alleyways like a mournful ghost.

The case consumed her daily thoughts, leaving her restless with suspicion. As she lay in bed, staring at the shadows dancing across her ceiling, her mind raced with images of Sebastian – his easy smile, handsome features, and how he seemed to captivate everyone around him effortlessly.

"Appearances can be deceiving," she reminded herself, her resolve hardening. "I won't let him charm his way out of this."

Detective Olivia's suspicions grew more substantial with each new piece of evidence, each whispered conversation, and each late-night revelation. She knew she was getting closer to unraveling Sebastian's secrets, but the truth remained just beyond her grasp, shrouded in darkness and doubt. As she continued her tireless pursuit for answers, the tension mounted, drawing her deeper into a tangled web of lies and deceit that threatened to ensnare them all.

Rain drizzled down the window panes of Lucy's café, blurring the view of the quiet street outside. The pattern of water droplets provided a soothing rhythm as Mrs. Thompson, Peter, and Lucy sat huddled in a corner booth, sipping steaming mugs of coffee to ward off the cold. The scent of freshly baked pastries wafted through the air, mingling with the aroma of damp earth and rain-soaked leaves.

"Detective Olivia stopped by today, again," Lucy confessed hesitantly, her fingers nervously tracing patterns on the worn wooden table. "She asked about Sebastian and said there were some inconsistencies she was looking into. She asked me if I knew anything about the other properties that Sebastian might purchase just before moving into the house. I told her I didn't hear about anything on sale recently, but she wasn't convinced."

"Really?" Peter replied, his eyebrows furrowing in concern as he leaned closer. "What kind of inconsistencies and what properties?"

"Something about his alibi, again... I don't know anything about any property," Lucy answered, her voice barely audible over the hushed murmur of other patrons. "And she mentioned finding a pattern in his behavior that seemed... off."

Mrs. Thompson glanced around nervously, expecting Sebastian to emerge from the shadows at any moment. "Do you think we've been too quick to trust him?" she asked, her voice trembling slightly. "I mean, he's always been so charming, but now that I think about it...."

"Maybe we've let our dislike for Gary cloud our judgment," Peter admitted, rubbing the back of his neck. "It's hard to believe that someone like Sebastian could be involved in whatever's happening."

"Everyone has secrets," Lucy murmured, her gaze distant as she stared out the rain-streaked window. "We should have looked deeper before giving him the benefit of the doubt."

The trio fell silent, each lost in their thoughts. Memories of their interactions with Sebastian swirled through their minds, and they began to re-examine every smile, every gesture, searching for the hidden meaning behind them.

"Remember that time he left his car unlocked?" Mrs. Thompson mused, her eyes widening in realization. "And the night he forgot to lock up his door? It all seems so careless now."

"Or calculated," Peter added darkly, his knuckles turning white as he gripped his coffee mug.

"Either way, we need to be more vigilant," Lucy declared, her jaw set with determination. "If something is going on, we can't afford to ignore it any longer."

The rain continued to fall outside, a relentless downpour obscuring their vision and leaving them uncertain. As they sat in the dimly lit café, the weight of their shared suspicions pressed down, binding them together in an uneasy alliance fueled by fear, doubt, and the desire for truth.

Detective Olivia stood in the pouring rain, her trench coat soaked as she examined the muddy ground outside the abandoned warehouse. The dilapidated warehouse building loomed ominously in the distance, starkly contrasting with the quaint town on its outskirts. Her mind raced with thoughts of Sebastian and the mounting evidence against him.

"That's the dump he bought?" asked Olivia, turning her head to Jenkins. "Yes, that shows up in his last name, but a different first name in the properties searches in the last six months," Jenkins said. He turns the searchlight and starts walking around the building. Olivia just stood there in the rain, and her face showed all kinds of disbelief. They didn't have a search warrant for the property. In reality, she could do nothing but walk around and watch. 'Is that place that Annie might be in?' she thought for a second, hoping to see something that would allow her to break into the house with a cause.

"Detective!" Officer Jenkins called out, his voice barely audible over the relentless downpour. "We found something."

Olivia hurried over to where Jenkins was crouched, her boots squelching in the mud. He held a crumpled piece of paper, the ink smudged from the rain but still legible.

"Look at this," he said, handing it to her. "It's a receipt from the local store with the card payment in Sebastian's name."

"Interesting," Olivia mused, her eyes narrowing as she studied the document. "Did you find anything else?"

"Actually, we did. A couple of witnesses saw Sebastian near this place last night." Jenkins hesitated before adding, "One of them even claims they saw him inside."

"Inside?" Olivia's heartbeat quickened at the thought. "Let's go check it out."

The air grew colder as they approached the building, and Olivia shivered involuntarily. She could feel the weight of the town's suspicions bearing down on her, suffocating her like the heavy raindrops that soaked her hair and dripped down her face.

"Here it is," Jenkins announced, pointing to a rusted padlock securing the door. "Looks like someone picked the lock."

"Probable cause to perform the search," said Olivia and drew her gun. "Stay sharp," Olivia warned as Jenkins pried the door open. They stepped inside, their flashlights cutting through the darkness to reveal the cavernous interior.

The barn in the warehouse style was filled with dust-covered crates, stacks of newspapers, and old furniture. As they ventured deeper, Olivia's flashlight fell upon a small table covered in photographs of Annie – taken from afar without her knowledge.

"Dammit," Olivia muttered, her heart sinking as she realized the discovery's significance. "He's been stalking her."

"Or worse," Jenkins added, his voice trembling with unease.

"Let's keep looking," Olivia said, her determination unwavering despite the dread that gripped her chest. She knew she couldn't let her emotions cloud her judgment, not when so much was at stake.

As they searched the warehouse, Olivia couldn't help but feel the town had betrayed her – that the people she'd sworn to protect had hidden their darkest secrets within these walls. She wondered if she could ever trust anyone again, knowing how easily Sebastian's charm and cunning had deceived them.

"Detective," the voice of the Jenkins crossed the warehouse, "You need to come over." Olivia turned around and followed the voice. Jenkins was standing next to the closed door that was hidden behind a hanging dirty black blanket. "Open it! Cut the lock," said Olivia and backed out when Jenkins grabbed the cutter. Lock dropped on the floor, and Jenkins grabbed the gun, slowly opening the door. The room was filled with sinister instruments – ropes, knives, and other tools meant for inflicting pain. The air was thick with tension as they stared at the horrifying scene before them, unable to shake the feeling that they were only beginning to uncover the truth about Sebastian's actions.

"God help us all," Olivia whispered, fear and uncertainty coursing through her veins as she grappled with the chilling reality of what they'd found. "What have we gotten ourselves into?"

Later the same night, Detective Olivia and her team were hard at work gathering evidence against Sebastian. They combed through this warehouse, dusting for fingerprints and collecting samples. The CSI team examined every inch of the property, searching for clues that could lead them closer to finding Annie.

"Detective, we found something interesting in the garage," one of the CSI technicians called to Olivia. She strode over, her eyes narrowing as she took in the scene before her.

"Looks like bloodstains on these tools," the technician explained, pointing to a set of pliers and a hammer covered in dark, dried splotches. "We'll have to run tests to confirm, but it doesn't look good."

"Keep me updated," Olivia instructed a grim determination settling over her features.

"All right, team. We have much evidence to sift through and not a moment to lose. Let's get to work."

As the officers dispersed to their various tasks, Olivia's thoughts turned to Annie, wondering what horrors she might be enduring at that very moment. She vowed to herself that she would leave no stone unturned in her quest to bring her home safely.

"Annie," she whispered into the encroaching darkness, "I promise you: we're going to find you wherever you are."

CHAPTER 6

The night was quiet and dark; only a few pale moons and stars could pierce the blackness. The summer breeze carries the scent of lilacs, dew, and freshly plucked grass, musky and sweet. Annie didn't hear Sebastian for a while now, 'he must be away,' she thought. Her mouth was dry, and the hot, bitter taste of the dirt echoed in her mouth. Annie's breaths came in sharp, ragged gasps as she crouched behind a rusty dumpster, her heart pounding. Her once elegant dress was now torn and muddied. The once vibrant crimson color faded to a dull, dirty brown. The cold air bit her cheeks, making them a painful pink shade. As she clutched her side, wincing from the throbbing pain where Sebastian had struck her, she couldn't shake the feeling that he had other intentions. Annie's thoughts raced with each passing second, the adrenaline coursing through her veins fueling her resolve. She knew that Sebastian would never let her go. As she replayed their interactions in her mind, she couldn't help but feel that there was something more sinister lurking beneath his charming facade.

"Sebastian," she whispered again, a steely resolve taking hold of her. "If you think you can control me, you're sorely mistaken."

Annie scrambled to her feet, desperate to find a chance to escape. The basement was dark and musty; she could feel the dampness clinging to her skin. She had one goal: freedom. She wiggled the basement door, and her big surprise door opened. She tiptoed around the corner, trying hard not to make any noise that could alert Sebastian. It felt like every nerve in her body was on high alert; she took shallow breaths and moved slowly, step by step, inching her way toward the kitchen door. Despite her fear, she managed to stay calm and collected and keep her wits about her. Her heart pounded in her ears as she felt around for the doorknob, silently praying it wouldn't be locked. With a sigh of relief, Annie found it, twisted it, and pushed open the door. As the door creaked open, the light from outside flooded into the room. Without hesitation, Annie ran outside into the darkness of night. Grateful for her luck, Annie stumbled across the yard, gritting her teeth as she felt each sharp pebble on her bare feet. She reached out to grab onto an old fence post to steady herself. Feeling the fear, emotions, and excitement from the adrenaline, she climbed over the fence and kept going into the dark.

The wind whipped around her, sending leaves dancing across the damp pavement as the storm clouds overhead threatened to unleash their fury. "Sebastian," she whispered under her breath, her voice trembling with both fear and anger. "What are your true intentions?" Through her pain, Annie's mind raced with possibilities, her manipulative nature pulling together scenarios like puzzle pieces. She couldn't afford to be naive; she needed to be one step ahead. She peeked out from behind the dumpster, scanning the deserted alleyway for any sign of Sebastian. It was too dark to see clearly, but she could see a tall figure approaching in the distance. Her heart leaped into her throat as she realized it wasn't him.

"Took you long enough." Annie heard a familiar voice coming from the alley.

Back at the station, Olivia spread all the evidence on her desk—photographs, witness statements, and now, the note. She began cross-referencing the information, searching for connections that might lead her closer to Annie. Her fingers danced across the keyboard, pulling up case files and articles on her computer screen.

"Sebastian received large sums of cash from an unknown account," she mumbled, her eyes narrowing in concentration. "And he's been making frequent visits to the same location—a warehouse on the outskirts of town." She looked up at Jenkins, her eyes wide. "But we've been there. Where else could he hold her? And where is he?"

"Let's analyze his behavior," Olivia suggested, her mind racing with determination. She recalled her recent interactions with Sebastian, observing how he'd acted when questioned about Annie's disappearance. His evasive gaze, the way he fidgeted with his hands—every detail seemed to point to guilt.

"Jenkins, remember when we first spoke with Sebastian?" she asked, her voice taut with intensity. "How he hesitated when we asked if he knew Annie?"

"Of course," he replied, nodding. "And the way he clenched his fists when we mentioned her name as if he was trying to hold something back."

"Exactly." She sighed, running a hand through her hair. "It's like he desperately wants to tell us something but can't. My gut tells me he's involved in this more than we ever could have imagined."

"Olivia," Jenkins said carefully, "you know I trust your intuition, but are you sure you're not letting your personal feelings cloud your judgment?"

"Annie's life could be at stake, Jenkins," Olivia snapped, her frustration rising. "I have to follow my instincts because time is running out."

She turned back to the evidence scattered across her desk, her mind churning with thoughts of Sebastian and Annie. An unsettling realization settled over her as she pieced together the puzzle before her. Sebastian might indeed be holding Annie captive, and Olivia was determined to uncover the truth.

"Let's talk to some witnesses again," she said, her voice steady and resolute. "There has to be something we've missed. We need to find Annie before it's too late." "Olivia, we're running out of time!" Jenkins shouted, his voice echoing through the dimly lit police station. The urgency in his tone sent a shiver down Detective Olivia's spine.

"Annie might be in grave danger," Olivia muttered, her eyes darting back and forth between the stacks of evidence piled high on her desk. "I know it. I can feel it." Her hands shook as she shuffled through the papers, searching for clues that could bring them closer to finding Annie.

"Damn it," Olivia cursed under her breath, her frustration mounting. She knew that if they didn't act fast, Annie's chances of survival would dwindle even further.

"Listen, Detective" - Jenkins leaned in close, his breath warm against her ear - "if what you think is true, then we need to get moving. We need to find her before Sebastian does something unthinkable."

Olivia's eyes flashed with determination as she met Jenkins' gaze. "I won't let her become another statistic, Jenkins," she vowed, her voice firm and steady.

"Neither will I," he replied, clapping a reassuring hand on her shoulder. Together, they sprang into action, ready to hunt down every possible lead in pursuing the truth.

As the first drops of rain began to fall, Detective Olivia and Jenkins pressed on, driven by their shared desire to save Annie from whatever nightmare awaited her.

"Time is not on our side," Olivia warned, her voice barely audible above the roar of the approaching storm.

The rain lashed against the car windows as Olivia and Jenkins drove through the town, seeking out potential witnesses in their desperate search for Annie. The air inside the vehicle was thick with determination, the urgency of their mission palpable.

"First up, the neighbor who saw Sebastian's car at the warehouse," Olivia said, her eyes narrowed as she focused on the road ahead. Jenkins nodded, pulling out his notepad and reading the address aloud. They pulled up to a small, unassuming house, its front yard littered with children's toys and garden tools, betraying the chaos within.

"Let's hope they know something useful," Jenkins muttered, stepping out of the car and holding his coat collar tight around his neck to shield himself from the onslaught of rain. Olivia followed suit, her gaze scanning the surroundings for any signs that might lead them closer to Annie.

As they approached the door, it swung open to reveal a weary-looking woman, her hair unkempt and dark circles underlining her eyes. "Detective Olivia and Officer Jenkins?" she asked, her voice trembling slightly. "I spoke to you on the phone earlier."

"Thank you for agreeing to meet with us," Olivia said, reassuringly smiling. "We just have a few questions about what you saw the night Annie disappeared."

"Of course, anything to help find that poor girl," the woman replied, ushering them inside and offering them seats at her cluttered kitchen table. As they questioned her about the events of that fateful night, Olivia couldn't help but notice the fear that seemed to grip the woman like a vice.

"Sebastian… he always gave me the creeps," she admitted, wringing her hands in her lap. "And when I saw his car outside that warehouse, I knew something was wrong."

"Did you see him interact with anyone else that night?" Jenkins asked, his pen poised over his notepad.

"No, but I heard him talking on the phone just before disappearing into the barn. He sounded… angry, almost frantic."

"Thank you," Olivia said, her mind racing with possibilities as they left the woman's home. "That might just be the lead we need to find Sebastian."

"Next, we should check out that diner where Annie was last seen before she vanished," Jenkins suggested, his eyes never leaving his notepad as they returned to the car.

The rain continued to pour as they questioned the diner's staff and patrons, piecing together a picture of Annie's final moments before her disappearance. But the cook, George, provided the most chilling revelation: "Sebastian came in here just after Annie left," he said, staring down at the countertop. "He looked like a man possessed, like he was hunting someone."

"Or something," Olivia muttered, exchanging a knowing glance with Jenkins.

"Thank you, George. Do you know where I can find him now? We searched his warehouse and the house. There is no sign of him anywhere".

"No, detective, I don't." George grabbed his butcher knife and sliced the meat on the board. "Actually, hold on, I think I saw him one day close to the church, in front of the abandoned house. The one that Mrs. Perry blessed her heart died in"

"Thank you, George. You helped us a lot. Let's go," said Olivia to Jenkins. It was time to confront the man at the center of this web of deceit. "Get the warrant to search his house. We have enough evidence that his involved. And check if He has a connection to Mrs. Perry's house."

Detective Olivia stood on the rain-soaked porch of Sebastian's house, her heart pounding with anticipation. The storm clouds above churned and growled, casting a shadow over the scene. It's been a week. Since the heavy rain flooded the town, it didn't look like that would ever end. Olivia took a deep breath and smelled the moisture na dozen in the air. 'it will be stormy tonight,' she thought before she made a move. A droplet of water slid down the curve of her cheek, but she paid it no mind. Her thoughts were already consumed by the case at hand. The detective had spent countless hours turning over every clue, fueled by her tenacity and empathy for the missing woman.

"Permission to search granted, Detective," announced Jenkins, showing Olivia the warrant. She nodded with determination, pushing open the door to Sebastian's home. The hinges creaked as the door swung wide, revealing a dimly lit interior.

"Thanks, Jenkins," she replied, stepping inside. "Keep an eye out here, just in case."

As Olivia's eyes adjusted to the darkness, she took in her surroundings. The living room was cluttered, with piles of newspapers and old books stacked haphazardly throughout the space. A musty odor hung in the air, a mixture of dampness and neglect.

She moved cautiously, her keen senses alert for anything that might lead her closer to finding Annie. Her fingers grazed the edges of a worn leather armchair, feeling the frayed stitching along its seams. She peered behind photographs on the walls, examining each one with care—Annie's smiling face haunted her thoughts, driving her forward.

"Where are you hiding your secrets, Sebastian?" Olivia muttered under her breath.

Then, in the corner of the room, she spotted a small, torn piece of paper peeking out from beneath a tattered rug. Her pulse quickened as she knelt to retrieve it, feeling the dampness of the floor seep through her jeans.

"Rescue Annie, $100k is yours," the note read in shaky, desperate handwriting. Olivia's heart leaped into her throat as she carefully examined the paper. The edges were frayed as though they had been hastily ripped from a larger sheet. She photographed the note with her phone, capturing every detail.

"Jenkins!" she called out, her voice tense with urgency. "I've found something."

"Let me see," he replied, rushing inside. Olivia handed him the note, watching as his face grew pale. "This could be what we need, Olivia."

"Rescue her?" asked Jenkins. "Is that real?"

"Annie might be in danger," she whispered, clenching her fists. "I won't rest until I've brought her to safety."

"Jenkins, did you check the basement?" Shouted to Jenkins. "There is no basement. I check everywhere. I don't see any door leading to the basement." said an officer. "Are you sure?" asked Olivia. "I guess not every house is made the same." Shown a little disbelieving, she decides to leave the house. "Gather everything we need and take all photos. Turn this place upside down, and let's meet later in the station to figure out what this note means. I'm done here." Olivia said, her eyes still on the torn piece of paper clutched in her hand. She could feel the weight of the words sinking into her chest, rattling around like loose change.

"Detective!" She heard just before she drove off the property. "You need to see this!" shouted one of the Officers that was searching the house. He stands on the front porch with something in his hands shaking".

"What is it?" asked Olivia with her heart beating fast and irregularly, as her breaths shallow.

"Photos, Annies' photos in some obscure basement, " said the officer.

"I've got a message, Detective, from the station. They linked Mrs. Perry's house to Sebastian. If he's holding Annie, that's going to be the place!" Jenkins almost shouted the whole sentence in one breath.

"Let's go!" Shouted Olivia, and her hope just restored. Maybe that's the place they find her. Perhaps this will be over for her and Annie.

They arrived at the abandoned house, the imposing structure looming ominously against the stormy skies. As they approached the door, Olivia felt a shiver run down her spine, an unnerving sense that they were walking straight into the lion's den. The door has a new lock, she noticed.

"Sebastian!" she barked, pounding on the door with clenched fists. "Open up! We need answers!"

The door creaked open, revealing a disheveled and agitated Sebastian. His eyes darted between Olivia and Jenkins, sensing the impending confrontation.

"Where is Annie?" Olivia demanded, her voice seething with anger and desperation.

"Detective, I don't know what you're talking about," Sebastian replied, feigning innocence but unable to hide the panic in his eyes.

"Enough games," Jenkins growled, stepping forward and towering over Sebastian. "We found your warehouse escape and searched your home. We have Annies photos. We know she's here! You're not fooling anyone."

"Sebastian," Olivia said, her voice soft but firm. "We know you're involved in Annie's disappearance. Tell us where she is, and maybe, just maybe, we can help you."

Sebastian hesitated, his eyes flicking back and forth between the two determined officers before him. The storm raged around them, the wind howling like a tortured soul as they awaited his answer. Sebastian's face contorted in frustration, a sharp contrast to the stoic façade he had maintained thus far. He stepped back, causing Detective Olivia and Jenkins to exchange a knowing glance. His posture slumped under the weight of the truth he carried within him.

"All right," he whispered, his voice cracking under the strain of his confession. "Annie is... She's locked away. But it's not what you think!"

"Explain yourself," Jenkins barked, his patience wearing thin.

Sebastian rubbed his temples and began pacing back and forth in the dimly lit foyer, the shadows of the storm outside casting eerie patterns across the walls. "She asked me to help her. I didn't know what else to do. She wanted to disappear from Gary's life, but she needed someone to take care of her while she figured out her next move."

"Where is she?" Olivia pressed, her heart pounding with anticipation.

"Downstairs. There's a hidden room," Sebastian replied, his voice trembling as if on the verge of tears. "Please, you have to understand. I was trying to protect her. I never meant for this to happen."

"Show us," Jenkins ordered, his stern gaze locking onto Sebastian as if daring him to try anything foolish.

As they followed Sebastian down a narrow staircase, the air grew colder and more oppressive, a suffocating heaviness that seemed to embody the gravity of their discovery. They reached the bottom of the stairs only to find themselves in a dimly lit hallway lined with grimy, cracked tiles. The air was damp and stale, like a forgotten tomb.

"Here," Sebastian said, pointing to a seemingly inconspicuous wall section. Upon closer inspection, Olivia noticed a faint outline of a hidden door. Her heart raced as she realized they were on the brink of a significant breakthrough.

"Open it," she demanded, her voice barely audible over the pounding of her own heart.

Sebastian hesitated for a moment before reluctantly pressing a hidden latch. The door creaked open, revealing a secret basement room. The walls were covered in chipping paint and mold, a single flickering light bulb casting ominous shadows across the space. At the center of the room were a rickety wooden chair, bed on the side, bathroom door, and small window, covered by paint and sealed tight.

"Annie?" Olivia called out cautiously, her eyes scanning every inch of the room.

"Detective, I swear she was here," Sebastian stammered, his face a mixture of confusion and fear. "I don't understand."

"Someone must have moved her," Jenkins speculated, his mind reeling with the implications of this new development.

"Or," Olivia said slowly, a chilling realization creeping into her thoughts, "she escaped."

As they stood there, contemplating the empty room and the tangled web of deception that had led them to this point, a gust of wind blew through the house, rattling the doors and windows like a warning from beyond. The storm outside continued to rage, its eerie melody echoing through the desolate halls as the detectives exchanged a glance filled with uncertainty.

What would happen next? Where was Annie now, and who could predict what twisted machinations she might set in motion? And how would Sebastian's role in this dark tale ultimately play out? As the unanswered questions swirled around them like the storm outside, one thing was clear: this mystery was far from over.

CHAPTER 7

The basement door creaked open as the group hesitated at the top of the stairs, their eyes slowly adjusting to the darkness below. Olivia led them down the rickety staircase, her heart pounding in her chest with every step she took. The air was damp, a musty scent invading their nostrils as they descended deeper into the gloomy abyss.

"Annie?" called Olivia, more for herself than Annie, her voice echoing off the concrete walls. "Annie, where are you?"

As they reached the bottom of the stairs, Olivia's flashlight beam flickered across the cluttered room: old furniture draped in dusty sheets, cobwebs clinging to the corners, and boxes piled high with forgotten memories. Their footsteps echoed on the cold floor as they searched through the shadows for any sign of their missing friend.

"Do you think she escaped?" pleaded Martha, her voice trembling with fear and concern. She glanced around nervously, her eyes darting from one darkened corner to the next.

"Guys, look at this," said Jenkins, pointing to a trail of muddy footprints on the floor. They followed the prints to a second small, windowless room in the back of the basement. Inside, they found a wooden chair knocked over and a length of frayed rope lying on the ground. Olivia's heart sank as she realized that Annie had been here, but where was she now?

"Annie!" screamed Olivia, her voice cracking with desperation. Her hands shook as she held the flashlight, casting erratic shadows on the walls. The others joined in, shouting Annie's name and combing through every inch of the basement, but their efforts were futile.

Olivia leaned against the wall, fighting back tears as she tried to make sense of the situation. "I don't understand," she whispered. "She has to be here somewhere."

"Maybe she got out," suggested one of the police officers, her voice still trembling. "Maybe she managed to escape and went for help."

"Or maybe someone moved her," Jenkins added with a hint of suspicion in his voice.

"Why and who?" asked Olivia, her eyes narrowing at the thought.

"Sebastian," said the officer quietly.

"Sebastian wouldn't hurt Annie," Martha said, shaking her head.

"Wouldn't he?" challenged Jenkins, raising an eyebrow. "We don't know what goes on behind closed doors. Maybe they had a falling out, or maybe he just snapped."

"Enough!" barked Olivia, cutting through the tension. "Speculating won't help us find her. Right now, we need to focus on where she could be."

The group fell silent, each lost in their thoughts as they contemplated the possibilities. They knew they couldn't give up on Annie, but the sinking feeling in their stomachs told them that something was terribly wrong. Their search for answers had only led to more questions, and as they stood in the cold, dark basement, they couldn't shake the unsettling feeling that time was running out.

The late afternoon sun cast long, eerie shadows across the town when Detective Olivia stood at the interrogation room door where Sebastian was held. This was the moment of truth. The air was heavy with anticipation, and a shiver ran down her spine as she considered the possibilities ahead.

Olivia paused momentarily on the door then, rapping her knuckles hard against the door. There was silence for a few heart-stopping seconds before it creaked open, revealing Sebastian's dark, striking eyes setting chained to the table.

"Sebastian, we need to talk," Olivia said, holding her fist on the holster. "We've been looking into Annie's disappearance, and some evidence has led us back to you. Where is she?"

Sebastian just sat there in silence. His face shows no emotion, maybe one, the feeling of the confusion that he was left behind, confusion about Annie's disappearance. She was just there in his basement a not long time ago, but now no one knows where she is, and everything is pointing at him. He felt a power for a second that only he knows all secrets about Annie, but then he reminded himself that he is clueless like Olivia, Jenkins, and all the other people in the town.

"Your fingerprints were found in the basement where Annie was last seen," Olivia explained, watching his face for any flicker of guilt or fear. "You were also the last person to see her alive."

"Of course," Sebastian replied, his tone still infuriatingly calm. "What do you want to know? That she was suffering? That she was hurt? That she was unhappy?"

"Did she suffer?" asked Olivia. "Suffer? How dare you ask about that. Everybody knows that her husband is a Monster!" shouted Sebastian.

"I'm not asking about her marriage! I'm asking if she suffered there in your basement. What did you do to her or with her body?" Olivia raised her voice, and her eyes became almost red from the rage she felt at that moment. She was ready to push Sebastian's face, but she held herself composed and hung there over Sebastian, like in the pause in the movie, to be prepared to play again and finish the game he played.

"I didn't do anything to her; I loved her, I couldn't watch her suffer with her husband, and I released her from her suffering," Sebastian spits pure raw emotion. He had tears in his eyes. "I loved her... I couldn't watch her be miserable every day, and I rescued her."

Olivia stepped back from the table and Sebastian and couldn't shake the nagging feeling that there was more to this story than met the eye. She glanced back at the mirror in the room. She knew that the town was watching, even if that room could only hold two people, she knew that the entire village would know what was said here quickly, and every second counted.

Olivia's thoughts raced. If Sebastian had killed Annie, where was her body? And why would he have done such a terrible thing? She couldn't help but wonder if perhaps Annie was still alive, hidden away somewhere by her captor.

"Sebastian," Olivia began, her voice wavering slightly as she tried to swallow her emotions. "Did you... Did you kill Annie?"

"Annie meant everything to me," Sebastian responded, his eyes downcast. "I would never hurt her."

"Then where the hell is she?" Olivia pressed, her grip tightening on the table.

"I helped her with something once, but I swear that's all. I don't know where she is," he insisted, his voice cracking slightly. "You have to believe me."

"Right now, Sebastian, the evidence isn't on your side," Olivia said gravely, her heart aching for the truth. Olivia's thoughts tumbled over one another like a stormy sea. She threw the documents she was holding in her hands and left the room. She wanted desperately to believe that Annie was still alive, that Sebastian had moved her somewhere else for reasons unknown. But as the cold metal door closed behind her, she couldn't shake the unsettling feeling that time was running out and that the answers they sought might be darker than any of them could have imagined.

An hour later, Olivia decided to give her another shot. "You know you can't hold him more than 48h here," said Jenkins quietly.

"If we can't find any hard evidence..."You mean body?" Olivia breaks his words plot. "I meant something tangible, even body." Jenkins tried to back up what he had just said. But Olivia waved her hands like she tried to escape a persistent fly.

The harsh fluorescent lights of the interrogation room cast unsettling shadows on the walls, highlighting every minor imperfection in the dingy gray paint. Sebastian sat slumped at the battered metal table, his wrists encircled by cold handcuffs that matched the chill in Olivia's bones as she prepared to resume the interrogation.

"Let's start from the beginning," Olivia said, her voice steady despite the turmoil within her. "Tell me everything you know about Annie's disappearance."

Sebastian lifted his head, his once-charming features now haggard and worn. "I've already told you, I don't know anything. I didn't hurt her."

"Then help me understand," Olivia pleaded, her eyes searching his for any sign of deceit. "Why were her fingerprints found in your basement? And what exactly did you help her with?"

Sebastian shifted uncomfortably in his seat. "We were moving some old furniture around, trying to clear out space for a new project," he explained, his gaze fixed on the scratched surface of the table. "Annie wanted to move an art studio down there."

"To your house? You don't have a basement!"

"To the empty house. I got it just for her."Whisper Sebastian.

"Did anyone see you two together that day?" Olivia asked, her mind racing through potential alibis and motives as she scribbled notes onto a paper pad.

"Gary might have," Sebastian replied hesitantly, avoiding Olivia's probing gaze. "But he was pretty busy with work stuff, so I don't know if he really noticed us."

"Speaking of Gary," Olivia continued, her tone hardening. "Were you aware of any problems between him and Annie? Any reason why he might have wanted her gone?"

"Gary never loved Annie," Sebastian responded, "but I don't think he would be able to kill her." Still, neither Olivia nor Jenkins wouldn't bet on that being the truth, especially since Sebastian's voice was full of anger and frustration creeping into the air. "He was hurting her all the time, but… This whole thing is insane. You're wasting time looking at us when you could be out there finding the person who took her!"

"Trust me, Sebastian, we're exploring every lead," Olivia assured him, though her doubts gnawed at the fringes of her mind. "But with her fingerprints in your basement and all Annie's belongings we found there, we know she was there. And she was there for a while. And What about that note we found - rescue her - 100k?"

"Annie is my friend," Sebastian insisted, desperation seeping through his words. "I would do anything to protect her. Please, just let me help find her."

Olivia stared at him for a long moment, the tension in the room as thick as the storm clouds that gathered outside the window. As the rain began to fall, heavy droplets splattering against the glass, she felt her frustration mounting. This interrogation was leading nowhere, and with each passing minute, Annie seemed farther and farther out of reach.

As Olivia left the interrogation room, the door clicking shut behind her, she couldn't help but feel that she was no closer to the truth. The investigation had hit yet another dead end, and with each fruitless lead, the hope of finding Annie alive grew dimmer and dimmer.

The wind whistled through the alley as Detective Olivia stepped over broken glass, her breath fogging in the crisp autumn air. The pale glow of the streetlight above illuminated the crumpled note clenched in her hand: "Rescue Annie, $100k is yours." It seemed too convenient. A shiver ran down her spine, not from the cold but from the nagging suspicion that something was amiss. She decided to go back to the abandoned warehouse and search all the little crevices around the block.

"Detective?" Officer Jenkins called out, his voice echoing off the damp brick walls. "I found something you might want to see."

Olivia followed the sound of his voice to the mouth of the alley, where a smudged fingerprint on a discarded newspaper caught her eye. She carefully retrieved a pair of latex gloves from her pocket and slipped them on, lifting the paper gingerly. The headline read: 'Local Woman Missing: Reward Offered.'

"Think this is related?" Jenkins asked, his brow furrowed.

"Could be," Olivia murmured, studying the fingerprint. "But let's keep looking."

As they continued their search, the scent of stale cigarettes and damp earth filled the air. Graffiti-covered dumpsters cast eerie shadows on the cracked pavement, adding to the unsettling atmosphere. Despite the discomfort, Olivia couldn't shake the thought of Annie, her face plastered on the newspaper clutched in her hand. She knew she had to find her, regardless of the dark forces at work.

"Officer Jenkins, I want you to canvas the area," she ordered, folding the newspaper and tucking it into her jacket pocket. "Interview anyone who might have seen or heard anything unusual."

"Right away, Detective," he replied, hurrying into the night.

Olivia decides to go back inside. The place was already searched, but maybe when the police left, he moved her back there? She hoped in her mind. The rusted metal gates creaked open, revealing a dark place littered with smashed crates and discarded syringes. She shuddered, knowing this place had witnessed countless lives destroyed by drugs and desperation.

"Annie, are you here?" she called out, her voice trembling slightly. Every instinct told her that walking further into the darkness was a terrible idea, but she pushed forward, propelled by her empathy for the missing woman.

As she stepped inside the warehouse, the cloying stench of mold and decay assaulted her senses. Piles of rotting debris made moving difficult, forcing her to pick her way carefully across the uneven floor. Rats scurried through the shadows, their beady eyes reflecting the weak moonlight filtering through shattered windows.

"Something's not right," Olivia muttered under her breath, shivering at the thought of what might have happened to Annie in this forsaken place.

A sudden noise caught her attention – the distant sound of footsteps echoing off the concrete walls. Her heart raced as she strained to listen, hoping against hope that Annie was somewhere nearby. But as the sound grew closer, Olivia realized it wasn't the desperate patter of a woman fleeing her captor but the heavy, deliberate steps of someone approaching with purpose.

"Who's there?" she demanded, her hand reaching instinctively for the gun holstered at her waist. "Show yourself!"

"Detective!" Jenkins's voice rang out, his breathless figure emerging from the darkness. "I've been looking all over for you! There's something we need to discuss."

"Discuss? What could possibly be more important than finding Annie right now?" Olivia snapped, frustration and fear bubbling up within her.

"Detective, I'm not sure how to say this, but I think we're being played," Jenkins said, swallowing hard as he met his steely gaze. "I spoke to some people back in town, and they don't believe this note is genuine. They think it's a setup to get us off the real trail."

"Damn it," Olivia muttered, her hands balling into fists. "We're running out of time."

Rain lashed against the window, casting a watery veil over Olivia's view of the desolate street below. The storm matched her mood – dark, turbulent, and unrelenting. She couldn't shake the gnawing fear that Annie was slipping further away with every passing moment.

"All right," she said to Jenkins, her voice taut with determination. "Let's go back to the beginning. We need to retrace our steps and examine every piece of evidence we have. There must be something we missed."

Jenkins nodded, his face mirroring his concern. They spread photographs, notes, and witness statements across the table, their hands brushing against each other as they searched for hidden connections or overlooked details.

They spent hours going through the evidence, photographs, and all evidence they took from all three places that Sebastian had ever been. But with each dead end, Olivia felt her frustration and desperation mounting. The chilling uncertainty of Annie's fate weighed heavily upon her, casting a shadow over every aspect of the investigation.

"Damn it!" she exclaimed, slamming her fist against the desk. "We're no closer to finding Annie than when we started! We're running out of time, Jenkins. What if we never find her? What if we're too late?"

"Detective," Jenkins said softly, touching her shoulder. "We won't give up until we've exhausted every lead. We'll find her. I promise you that."

But as the storm continued to rage outside, mirroring the chaos within Olivia's heart, she couldn't help but wonder if some mysteries were destined to remain unsolved.

CHAPTER 8

Rain lashed against the windows of the police station, casting a gloomy pallor over the bustling interior. A lone figure stepped through the double doors, water dripping from her sodden coat. Shivering, Annie pulled her scarf tighter around her neck as she scanned the room for a friendly face. Her heart pounded in her chest like a caged bird seeking escape. This was the moment she had been both dreading and anticipating for some time now.

"Excuse me," Annie said hesitantly to a uniformed officer passing by. "Please, I just want to speak to Detective Olivia," Annie whispered, her voice barely audible over the growing commotion.

"Take a seat, ma'am," the officer replied dismissively, barely glancing in her direction before hurrying off on some seemingly urgent task. As if she were invisible, the other officers did their business, paying her no mind.

Her hands trembled as she clutched at the frayed ends of her scarf, her fingers numb from the cold and fear. She felt the weight of her dark secret bearing down upon her, threatening to suffocate her if she couldn't find someone to share her burden. And then, like a beacon of hope in this cold, uncaring place, Detective Olivia emerged from the back office.

"Annie?" Olivia's eyes widened with surprise as recognition dawned. "Is that really you?"

"Detective Olivia," Annie whispered, her voice cracking. "Please... I need your help."

Instantly, Olivia crossed the room, shielding Annie from the curious gazes of her colleagues and the emerging meddlers. "Come with me," she urged gently, leading her down a quiet hallway away from the chaos, leading her into a small, dimly lit interrogation room. The door closed behind them, muffling the noise from the busy station. Olivia gestured for Annie to sit down, her gaze filled with concern.

"Tell me what happened. Are you OK? Where have you been?" Olivia prompted gently, her voice low and soothing.

Annie swallowed hard, feeling as though her throat had been lined with sandpaper. She looked down at her lap, her fingers wringing the hem of her coat. "It's Gary," she began, her voice barely audible over the harsh drumming of rain against the windowpane. "He... he hurts me."

"Take your time," Olivia encouraged, her hand brushing against Annie's in a moment of comfort.

"Everyone knew," Annie began, her voice barely above a whisper. "People in this town disregarded what Gary was doing to me. Every day, I walk on eggshells around him, terrified that one wrong move will set him off." As the words tumbled forth, Annie's voice grew stronger; her pain and fear transformed into anger. "At first, it was just the cruel words, you know? The kind that cut deep, leaving invisible scars. But then it escalated. He would slap me, punch me, throw me to the ground like I was nothing more than a rag doll."

"Annie," Olivia whispered, tears welling in her eyes as she listened.

"Sometimes, when he'd had a few too many, he would force himself on me, claiming it was his right as my husband. And the worst part is, I believed him. I thought this was what marriage was supposed to be."

As Annie continued her story, Detective Olivia could see the pain and fear in her eyes. Her voice quavered as she spoke of Gary's relentless abuse - broken glass, busted knuckles, barely healed cuts and bruises that stretched across both arms. The detective felt her own heart wrenching with each new detail of Annie's suffering, watching as tears streamed down her face.

"Mrs. Thompson from next door saw him hit me many times," she continued, her voice growing stronger as she spoke. "But she just closed her curtains and pretended not to notice; every single time." Annie almost spelled that last words. "He almost killed me the last time," Annie managed to choke out. "That's when I finally knew... This wasn't right."

The air in the room seemed to grow colder as if the storm outside had seeped through the walls and settled around them. Shadows cast by the flickering light danced on Annie's face, revealing a haunted look as she continued. "But it wasn't just Gary," she said, her voice cracking with a mixture of anger and disbelief. "It was this whole damn town."

"Go on," Detective Olivia urged softly, her eyes narrowing in an effort to understand.

"People here, they know what's been happening," Annie confessed, her eyes darting around the room as though searching for hidden witnesses. "I've seen how they stare at me when I walk down the street, how they quickly look away when I catch their eye. They whisper behind my back but never dare to say anything to my face. It's like they're afraid to acknowledge the truth."

As she spoke, images of the small town came flooding into Olivia's mind: the quaint row of houses along Maple Street, the cozy diner where locals gather every morning for breakfast, and the silent church that loomed over the community like a watchful guardian.

Annie;'s voice trembled with hurt, and Olivia could see the weight of betrayal crushing her spirit.

"Annie, I'm so sorry," Olivia said, her hand instinctively reaching out to offer comfort.

"Everyone just looked the other way, pretending they didn't see or hear anything. It's like this town has a sickness, cancer that nobody wants to admit is there. And I..." Annie swallowed hard, her eyes glistening with unshed tears. "I couldn't take it any longer."

Detective Olivia's jaw tightened, a flicker of rage igniting within her. She thought of the countless victims she had encountered throughout her career – those who had been silenced by fear and indifference – and knew that Annie's story was all too familiar.

"And then Sebastian..."

"We know; we found the basement. We know he was holding you there. We were looking everywhere; we thought you…"

"I did escape." Annie stopped her in the middle of the sentence.

Olivia reached across and pulled Annie into a tight embrace, letting her tears fall against her chest. After a while, she released the trembling woman and grabbed two tissue boxes from behind her desk before gently pressing one into Annie's hand."It's OK now," she murmured softly as they both wiped their tears away. "We'll get through this together. Annie, I promise you," Detective Olivia said, her voice firm and resolute, "I will do everything in my power to ensure justice is served. No one should have to go through what you've experienced.

"Maybe I brought this all to myself, that I didn't react soon enough?"

"Annie, what happened to you is not your fault. The people in this town, they failed you. They should have protected you, supported you – but they didn't." Olivia's voice rang with conviction, her words a balm for Annie's wounded heart. "But we can make sure that Gary pays for what he's done and help you find a way to heal."

"Th-therapy?" Annie stammered, the word foreign on her tongue.

"Yes," Olivia confirmed, her voice steady and reassuring. "There are professionals who specialize in helping people like you who have experienced trauma and abuse. They can help you reclaim your life and find your way back to yourself."

Annie looked up at Detective Olivia, her eyes filled with a tentative hope that hadn't been there before. At that moment, she dared to believe that maybe, just maybe, she could escape the nightmare that had been her life for far too long.

A gentle breeze rustled the leaves of the trees lining the sidewalk as Annie approached her sanctuary in the heart of town – Lucy's café. The warm brick exterior, adorned with climbing ivy, exuded timeless charm and comfort. Large windows revealed a cozy interior filled with worn wooden tables and mismatched chairs, inviting patrons to linger for hours over their meals.

When she entered the door, Annie was enveloped in the familiar, comforting scent of freshly brewed coffee mingling with the subtle sweetness of cinnamon pastries. It was here that she found solace in the hollows of her healing journey, and it was Lucy who had become her beacon of hope amid the storm.

"Annie! You're just in time for a fresh batch of scones," Lucy called out from behind the counter, her voice warm and welcoming. Her apron was smudged with flour, evidence of her dedication to the homemade treats that graced the glass display case.

"Sounds perfect, Lucy. Thank you," Annie replied, her eyes scanning the room for a quiet corner where she could sit undisturbed.

"Take your usual spot, dear. I'll bring them over," Lucy said, understanding Annie's unspoken need for privacy.

As Annie settled into her favorite nook by the window, she couldn't help but feel a sense of gratitude for this safe haven and the friend who had created it. Lucy had offered her a place to escape the townspeople's prying eyes and was a source of unwavering support throughout her ordeal.

"Here you go, Annie," Lucy said, placing a plate of warm scones and a steaming cup of coffee on the table. "I added some extra blueberries in your batch, just like you like them."

"Thank you, Lucy. That's really sweet of you," Annie replied, touched by the gesture.

"Of course. And if you need anything else, just let me know," Lucy assured her before retreating to the counter, leaving Annie with her thoughts.

Annie took a moment to savor the sweet aroma of her coffee and the buttery warmth of the scone before taking a bite. The flavors felt like an embrace, reminding her that she was not alone in her quest for healing. As she savored each morsel, her thoughts drifted back to her therapy sessions, reflecting on the progress she had made thus far.

I can do this, she told herself, bolstered by the unwavering support of Detective Olivia and her friends. I am no longer alone in my journey.

The café buzzed around her with quiet conversations and the clatter of dishes, yet it remained a sanctuary for Annie as she worked to rebuild her life. With each visit, she found solace and strength in the familiar surroundings and the comforting presence of her friend Lucy.

And as she sat there, sipping her coffee and watching the world go by through the window, Annie allowed herself to believe that a brighter future awaited her.

Annie's fingers trembled as she clutched the steaming mug of coffee, her breath mingling with the swirls of steam that rose to meet her. The bitter cold outside seemed to recede into a distant memory as she sat in the warm embrace of the café, surrounded by the soft sounds of laughter and quiet conversation.

"Annie," Lucy said gently, touching her friend's quivering shoulder. "You know you can talk to me, right? About anything."

Annie looked up from her mug, her eyes glistening with unshed tears. She hesitated for a moment, then sighed, her shoulders slumping as if releasing a great weight. "I just... I didn't realize how much everything would hurt, you know? Coming back here, seeing all those familiar faces..."

As she spoke, Annie felt the ache in her chest intensify as though a vice was tightening around her heart. Her hands clenched into fists, nails digging into her palms as she grappled with the flood of emotions threatening to overwhelm her.

"Annie," Lucy murmured, her voice full of compassion. "It's okay to feel hurt, angry, even betrayed. What happened to you was not your fault, and it's important to remember that."

"Sometimes," Annie admitted, her voice barely audible, "I can't help but think that maybe I deserved it. That maybe I brought it upon myself."

"Annie, no," Lucy interjected, her voice firm yet gentle. "You are not to blame. You deserve so much better than what you've been through."

"Lucy," Annie choked out, her eyes brimming with fresh tears. "Thank you. Thank you for being here for me, for believing in me."

"Of course, Annie. We're friends, aren't we?" Lucy smiled softly, giving Annie's hand a reassuring squeeze.

As the two women sat there, the café's cozy atmosphere seemed to wrap around them like a quilt, offering a sense of security and belonging that Annie had long been denied. She felt her chest constrict with gratitude as she watched Lucy's warm smile lighting up the room, a beacon of hope in the midst of her evil thoughts.

"Lucy," Annie whispered, her voice heavy with emotion. "I want to move forward, I really do. But sometimes it feels like I'm trapped in a web of my own making, unable to break free."

"Annie," Lucy said softly, leaning in so their foreheads nearly touched. "Healing is a journey, and it won't happen overnight. You will have good days and bad days, but you're not alone. We're here for you every step of the way."

"Thank you, Lucy," Annie murmured, "There is one more thing I have to do here," the fog of despair lifting ever so slightly as she allowed herself to lean on her friend's unwavering support. Lucy thought for a second that these last words sounded like the ominous course rather than just something on the shopping list, but she brushed off the thoughts and forgot about that moment later.

And so, with each tear shed and each word spoken, Annie found herself inching closer to the light at the end of the tunnel, her heart slowly mending under the watchful gaze of those who cared for her most.

The therapist's office was warm and inviting, decorated with soft pastel colors and filled with the scent of lavender and vanilla. As Annie settled into the comfortable armchair, the therapist, Dr. Roberts, introduced herself and explained the techniques they would use to help her heal.

"Annie, we'll be using a combination of cognitive behavioral therapy and trauma-focused therapy to address both your thought patterns and the emotional impact of your experiences," Dr. Roberts said, her voice soothing and professional. Annie nodded, the knot of anxiety in her chest loosening ever so slightly as she stared out at the sun-dappled square. She knew the road ahead would be fraught with obstacles, but with each step she took, she felt more determined than ever to break free from the chains that had bound her for so long.

"You're stronger than you think, Annie," Dr. Roberts replied, his gaze steady and unwavering. "And I do not doubt you'll continue to grow and heal, one day at a time."

"Thank you, Dr. Roberts," she said quietly, her voice barely audible above the din of the market below. "I couldn't have come this far without your guidance."

"How has your week been?"

"Better, actually," Annie replied, settling into the cushions as she gazed at the bustling market below. "I've started volunteering at the community center, helping with the after-school program for kids. It's given me a sense of purpose."

"Ah, that's wonderful news," Dr. Roberts said, nodding approvingly. "Finding meaningful activities can be incredibly therapeutic. How are you navigating the challenges of being back in the town?"

Annie hesitated, her fingers twisting the hem of her skirt as she recalled the whispers and stares that seemed to follow her everywhere she went. "It's not easy," she admitted. "There are times when I feel like a stranger in my own home, haunted by the memories of what happened. But I'm learning to face those fears, one day at a time."

"Facing our fears is an essential part of healing," Dr. Roberts agreed, scribbling a note on his pad. "And remember, you don't have to do it alone. Your friends are there to support you."

"Lucy has been a rock," Annie said, a small smile tugging at the corners of her lips. "She's always there when I need someone to talk to or just a shoulder to cry on."

"Social support can be a powerful tool in overcoming trauma," Dr. Roberts remarked, his eyes soft with empathy. "Allow yourself to lean on those who care about you, and don't hesitate to reach out when you need help."

As she left the office, Annie's heart swelled with newfound determination, bolstered by the knowledge that, with the help of her friends and therapy, she was slowly but surely rebuilding the life she had lost. The shadows of her past may still linger, but as she walked through the town square under the golden afternoon light, she knew that she held the power to forge her own path toward a brighter future. But Dr. Roberts felt different this time. It's almost like she felt some undeniable lies under the pretend face of the traumatized victim.

The sun dipped low in the sky, casting a warm orange glow over the quaint houses lining the town's cobblestone streets. Annie stood on Lucy's doorstep, her heart pounding with anticipation and anxiety. She took a deep breath, inhaling the sweet scent of freshly baked bread mingling with the floral aroma of the nearby flower shop.

"Ready for our girls' night?" Lucy asked, opening the door with a bright smile.

Annie nodded, her throat tightening with emotion as she embraced her friend. "More than you know," she replied, her voice barely above a whisper. As they entered the cozy living room, the walls adorned with hand-painted canvases and colorful tapestries, Annie felt an unfamiliar warmth envelop her. It was the feeling of belonging, of safety – something she had been craving for so long.

"Promise me something," Lucy said, her gaze locked onto Annie's. "Promise me that you'll keep fighting, no matter how hard it gets. That you'll never give up on yourself or your dreams."

"I promise," Annie said, her voice choked with emotion as she sealed the pact with her friend.

Later that night, as the sun finally disappeared behind the horizon and the room was bathed in the soft glow of candlelight, Annie took a step back to admire her vision board, her heart swelling with pride and hope. The images before her eyes shimmered like stars in a vast and infinite sky, each a beacon guiding her toward a new beginning.

"Thank you, Lucy," she whispered, feeling a weight lift off her shoulders. "For everything."

"Always, Annie," Lucy replied, wrapping an arm around her friend. "We're in this together, remember?"

As they stood there, shoulder to shoulder, their bond only grew stronger, Annie felt as if she could conquer the world. With each passing day, she was reclaiming the pieces of herself that had been lost, forging a new identity from the ashes of her past. And though the journey ahead would undoubtedly be filled with challenges and setbacks, she knew she had the strength – and the support – to face them head-on.

Beneath the star-studded sky, Annie dared to dream of a future unburdened by fear or pain, a life filled with love, laughter, and adventure. And as the first whispers of dawn kissed the horizon, she vowed to make those dreams a reality, one step at a time, just not with the person that stood for her all this time.

CHAPTER 9

The heavy oak doors of the courtroom swung open, each creaking an audible reminder of the trial's importance. The somber atmosphere was tense, as if the air knew what was at stake. Rigid wooden benches lined the gallery, filled with silent spectators who had come to see justice served. At the front of the room, the judge's bench towered over the proceedings, its mahogany surface polished to a sheen that reflected the seriousness of the matter.

The bailiff called out, "All rise!" and the assembly in the courthouse rose in unison. The imposing figure of the judge entered, his black robe billowing around him like a cape of authority. As he took his seat, the silence in the room was palpable, broken only by the shuffling of feet and the barely audible whispers of nervous anticipation.

"Bring in the witness," commanded the judge, his voice deep and resonant, echoing throughout the chamber. The doors opened once more, and Annie stepped into the courtroom. She moved with quiet confidence, and her gaze was steely and determined. A fierce resolve had replaced her once timid demeanor. The transformation was evident in every step she took toward the witness stand.

As Annie sat down, the prosecutor began his questioning. The words flowed from her lips with calm certainty, recounting the years of abuse she had endured at Gary's hands. The hushed murmurs of the onlookers underscored the gravity of her testimony. Each vivid detail she shared made it increasingly clear how much she had suffered.

"Could you please describe the day your husband first hit you?" the prosecutor asked, his tone gentle yet probing.

Annie swallowed hard, memories of that fateful day flooding her senses: the sharp sting of the slap, the coppery taste of blood in her mouth, and the icy fear gripped her heart. "It was raining," she began, her voice barely a whisper but growing stronger with each word. "I remember the sound of the raindrops pounding on the roof, like bullets from an unseen enemy."

She took a deep breath and continued. "He was shouting at me, his voice filled with rage. He struck me that I fell to the ground. I was in shock - I didn't know what to do or how to defend myself. He kept hitting me until I felt like I couldn't take it anymore."

Her words hung in the air as tears rolled down her cheeks. She wiped them away and mustered up her courage once more before continuing her testimony.

"He told me he would kill me if I ever tried to leave him," she said softly. "That's when I knew I had to get out of there no matter what." Annie's voice grew stronger and more determined with every sentence as she recounted the brave steps she had taken to free herself from Gary's control and seek justice for all he had done to her.

The courtroom was absolutely silent as Annie finished speaking, a powerful reminder of how much courage it had taken for her to speak out against her abuser after so many years of suffering in silence. Everyone held their breath as Annie continued to chronicle the terror she had lived with for so long. The jurors' faces reflected a mixture of empathy and shock, their eyes never leaving her as they absorbed the weight of her words.

Across the room, Gary sat in the defendant's chair, his once-confident posture now wilted under the scrutiny of his crimes. As Annie testified, his face contorted into a mask of barely restrained fury, unable to refute the undeniable truth spoken by the woman he had tormented for years.

"Annie, do you believe that your husband, Gary, is capable of change?" the prosecutor asked, his gaze fixed on her expectant face.

She took a deep breath, her eyes locking onto Gary's. "No," she said firmly, her voice unwavering. "For years, I prayed for change, but my prayers went unanswered. I realized that some people are incapable of it."

"Annie, I love you. I didn't mean it!" Shouted Gary from the defendant's desk.

"Silence!" Shouted Judge, "I will not tolerate interruptions! One more outburst, and I will hold you in contempt of court!"

The courtroom was filled with stunned silence as everyone processed the unexpected confession.

"I don't love you anymore," murmured Annie.

Her words echoed through the courtroom, the impact clear on the judge and jury alike. Her testimony would be crucial in determining the consequences of Gary's abusive behavior.

The scene in the courtroom was etched with unshakable clarity: Annie, standing tall and resolute, no longer a victim but a survivor; Gary, a broken man forced to confront the reality of his actions; and the jury, who held power to decide his fate.

The courtroom hushed as the prosecutor approached Annie again, a steely determination evident in his eyes. The air hung heavy with tension and anticipation, the scent of old wood and worn leather permeating the room. Sunlight streamed through the windows, casting long shadows across the floor. Gary's jaw was clenched tightly, his knuckles white from gripping the table before him.

"Thank you, Annie," the prosecutor said softly, allowing her to collect herself before continuing. "Do you believe that Gary poses a threat to you if he is allowed to go free?"

Annie's eyes met Gary's once more, hardened by years of torment, and she nodded resolutely. "Yes, I do. He would stop at nothing to regain control over me and continue his pattern of abuse."

As she spoke, the room seemed to shrink, the gravity of her words pressing down on those present. The jurors leaned forward in their seats, captivated by the raw emotion in her voice. Outside, the wind howled and rattled the windowpanes, but within the courtroom, all was still.

Gary's face grew redder and sweatier as he fought to contain his anger. His chest rose and fell with each heaving breath, the veins in his neck straining against his skin. It starkly contrasted from earlier, when he had professed his love. Everyone could see that this was now his game.

"Thank you, Annie. No further questions," the prosecutor said, stepping back from the witness stand. The judge looked down at his notes, his face a mask of solemn contemplation. "Next witness."

Mrs. Thompson looked around the courtroom as Annie completed her testimony, her heart aching in sorrow for all that had been lost and stolen from this young girl she'd known. She remembered all the days of turmoil, how Anne's face was often shadowed with fear and anxiety whenever Gary entered the room, yet he seemed to revel in it - his aura carrying an undeniable air of arrogance as if supposing that no one would challenge him on his behavior despite it being utterly wrong.

"Mrs. Thompson, as a witness to these horrific events, can you attest that Annie was subjected to regular physical abuse from Gary?"

Mrs. Thompson nodded solemnly and spoke up in a clear voice: "I saw it every day for years – the bruises on her body, the fear in her eyes." She took a deep breath and continued firmly: "Annie suffered greatly at his hands, but I knew she'd never stand for such treatment indefinitely; eventually, something had to give - thank goodness now is that time." Her words rang out with conviction throughout the courtroom before turning towards Annie with an expression of admiration tinged with sorrow.

Mrs. Thomas' face twisted with rage as she recalled Gary's violence and abuse towards Annie. "I've seen her cowering against the wall, tears running down her cheeks after Gary had whipped her with his belt," she said through gritted teeth, her voice shaking with fury. "We all watched what he did to her and yet did nothing to stop him - I can still hear her muffled cries echoing in my ears." Mrs. Thomas couldn't contain the anger that boiled within her.

"Thank you, Mrs. Thompson; I have no further questions."

As the courtroom buzzed with whispered conversations and the rustle of paper, Annie felt a swell of determination rise within her. She had faced her abuser head-on, refusing to let him escape the consequences of his actions. With each word she spoke, she felt herself reclaiming a piece of her life that Gary had taken from her.

Over the course of the trial, the courtroom became a battleground for Annie and Gary's conflicting motivations. Witnesses were called for several hours daily, testimonies were heard, and evidence was presented. The atmosphere was tense as the weight of justice hung on every detail.

Annie could feel the anticipatory gaze of the jury, their eyes flicking back and forth between her and Gary, seeking to discern truth from falsehood. Morning light filtered through the high windows, casting long shadows across the gallery, like fingers reaching out to grasp the scales of justice.

"Ms. Miller," the defense attorney addressed Annie, his voice smooth, like oil on water. "You claim that my client physically abused you throughout your marriage. Can you be more specific about these incidents?"

Annie hesitated, swallowing hard before meeting his probing gaze. "Yes," she whispered, her voice barely audible. She took a deep breath, steadying herself before launching into a vivid account of the abuse she had endured. With each detail she shared, the room collectively held its breath as if the air recoiled at the horrors she described.

As she recounted one particularly brutal episode, Annie noticed a juror in the front row, a middle-aged woman with tightly coiled hair, flinching and averting her eyes. It was a small victory but fueled Annie's resolve to continue.

"Furthermore," Annie continued, her voice growing stronger, "his constant need for control extended beyond physical violence. He isolated me from my friends and family, monitored my every move, and demeaned me at every turn."

Gary maintained an impassive facade throughout her testimony, though the occasional twitch of his jaw betrayed his internal struggle. His hands gripped the edges of the defendant's table, knuckles whitening with the effort of restraint.

"Objection!" the defense attorney interjected suddenly, his tone sharp and accusatory. "Your Honor, the witness is speculating about my client's intentions."

"Overruled," the judge replied sternly. "The witness is recounting her own experiences and observations."

"Once, after I tried to leave him, he dragged me back into our house by my hair, threw me onto the floor, and kicked me repeatedly while yelling that I was nothing without him," Annie recounted, her voice breaking.

"Thank you, Mrs. Miller," the prosecutor said gently, pausing to give her a moment to compose herself. "We know this is difficult, but your testimony is crucial in ensuring Gary faces the consequences of his actions."

Annie nodded, wiping away the tears that had begun to fall. She knew reliving these dark memories was necessary and would not let her pain be in vain. With renewed determination, she continued her testimony, resolute in her pursuit of justice.

Annie couldn't help but relish in the small triumph, allowing herself a brief moment of satisfaction before refocusing on her testimony. The trial continued each day, a test of endurance, as both sides presented their cases.

Nights were tough for Annie, as memories of her abuse haunted her dreams. She tossed and turned, her mind refusing to rest. But each morning that dawned, she found the strength to face another day in court.

As the days wore on, the emotional toll of the trial began to show on Annie's face, her eyes shadowed by dark circles and her once-youthful features etched with lines of exhaustion. But her gaze also had a steely determination, a fire that refused to be extinguished.

The courtroom was bathed in a soft, diffused light streaming from the tall windows lining one side of the room. Hushed murmurs ebbed and flowed through the gallery like a gentle tide as the spectators took their seats, anticipation palpable. The dark wood-paneled walls lent an air of solemnity to the proceedings, while the very structure of the room, with its raised platform for the judge, witness stand, and rows of seating for the jury, spoke of order and the weight of justice.

The heavy door at the back of the courtroom creaked open, and all eyes turned to see Annie enter, her steps measured and steady, despite the trembling she felt within. Her pale blue dress seemed to float around her like a delicate cloud, the color chosen to evoke innocence and vulnerability. A simple silver locket hung around her neck, the only piece of jewelry she wore - a quiet reminder of the life she once had before Gary's abuse began.

Annie's face bore the evidence of sleepless nights and the emotional turmoil that had taken hold of her during the trial. Though her eyes were rimmed with red and shadowed by exhaustion, they held within them a fierce determination that could not be ignored. Though slender and seemingly fragile, her shoulders were squared and held firm, refusing to bow under the weight of her past.

As she made her way to the witness stand, she could feel the spectators' gaze boring into her, studying her every move, weighing the truth of her words before they were even spoken. They knew her story, but she would make sure they heard it again and understood the depths of the suffering she had endured.

Her hands gripped the sides of the witness stand, the excellent wood offering a small measure of comfort as she steadied herself for the testimony ahead. As she looked out over the sea of faces, her eyes locked onto Gary's, and for a moment, the world seemed to fall away. The anger, pain, and fear that had long simmered within her now rose like a tide, threatening to drown her in its depths.

But she held fast, the ghost of a smile touching her lips as she prepared to speak. This was her moment of truth, her chance to reclaim the power that had been stolen from her, and she would not falter in her quest for justice.

The courtroom was alive with the rustle of papers, the murmurs of hushed conversations, and the occasional cough breaking the tense silence. The air hung heavy, a mixture of stale breath and the faint scent of disinfectant lingering from the previous day's cleaning. The walls seemed to bear witness to countless stories of lives changed forever, their once pristine white paint now mottled with age and exposure to the unrelenting passage of time.

A single bulb overhead cast sharp shadows across the room, highlighting the solemn faces of the jury members as they studied Annie. She could feel their scrutiny, feel the weight of their expectations bearing down upon her. But she would not be deterred; she had come this far and would see justice served.

As she stepped down from the witness stand, her hands no longer trembled, and her spine remained straight. It was as if recounting the details of her abuse had empowered her, giving her the strength to face her abuser head-on and reclaim her life.

As she walked past Gary, their eyes locked briefly – hers filled with defiance and newfound resilience, his swirling storm of anger and disbelief. In that instant, Annie realized that she had succeeded in breaking free from his control, and nothing could ever hold her down again.

The air in the courtroom felt thick with anticipation as Annie's testimony reverberated through the minds of all present. The jury members exchanged glances amongst themselves, their faces a mixture of sympathy and skepticism. Some clung to their notepads, scribbling furiously as they dissected her words; others stared intently at Annie, trying to gauge the truth behind her sorrowful eyes.

The judge, a stern, middle-aged man with a graying beard and piercing blue eyes, leaned back in his chair. He took a deep breath, his eyes flicking between Annie and Gary, seeming to weigh the gravity of her accusations against the stoic face of the accused.

"Miss Miller, your request for a restraining order has been noted," the judge announced, his voice steady and authoritative. "I will grant a recess for the court to review the necessary documentation."

The gavel struck, echoing throughout the room like thunder. As the room emptied, murmurs and whispers filled the air, punctuated by the faint sound of raindrops pelting against the courtroom windows.

Annie sat down, her fingers tapping anxiously on the wooden armrest. She knew securing a restraining order was no easy feat – it hinged on the court's assessment of her credibility and the severity of the abuse she had endured. Her mind raced with the memories of countless doctors' visits, late-night calls to friends, and desperate cries for help. She knew she could provide the evidence needed – but bringing it to light meant reliving her darkest moments again.

"Your Honor," her lawyer began when the court reconvened, "we have submitted medical records and witness statements demonstrating a pattern of abuse inflicted upon my client by the defendant. We respectfully request that a restraining order be granted to protect Miss Miller from further harm."

The judge's eyes scanned the documents before him, and his brow furrowed in concentration as he considered their implications. The room fell silent, the only sound of the ticking clock on the wall and the persistent rain tapping against the glass. The trial continued, each day presenting new challenges and revelations. But through it all, Annie stood tall, her resolve unwavering. And when the verdict was finally delivered, it was clear that her testimony had indelibly impacted the judge, jury, and even Gary himself.

"Mr. Gary Miller," the judge intoned solemnly, "based on the evidence presented, I am granting a restraining order against you. You are hereby prohibited from coming within 500 feet of Miss Annie Miller or attempting to contact her. Failure to abide by these conditions will result in immediate arrest and possible imprisonment. And over the emotional damages caused by repeated abuse, $1,500.000 for the plaintive."

The gavel struck again, sealing Gary's fate with an air of finality. He clenched his jaw tightly, his eyes ablaze with fury as they bored into Annie's soul.

Annie, however, refused to cower beneath his gaze. Her heart pounded wildly in her chest, adrenaline coursing through her veins as the realization took hold – she had done it. She had faced her abuser and won, securing her safety and others who might have suffered at his hands. She won. She woke more than she had planned...

As the courtroom began to empty, the gray clouds outside gave way to golden streaks of sunlight. At that moment, Annie felt the warmth of hope wash over her, illuminating the path toward a future free from fear and torment.

The courtroom door swung open, releasing Annie into the cool embrace of the marble hallway. In an instant, she felt a sense of liberation and transformation wash over her. The heavyweight of Gary's abuse seemed to dissipate, replaced by the knowledge that she had taken control of her life once more. A soft smile graced her lips as she stepped away from the darkness of the courtroom into the corridor bathed in natural light.

"Annie," Lucy called out, walking toward her with an expression of relief and admiration. "You did it."

"Thank you, Lucy," Annie responded, feeling the warmth of gratitude fill her chest. "I couldn't have done it without you."

"Remember, this is just the beginning," she said, placing a supportive hand on her shoulder. "But you've taken a significant step toward your freedom."

Annie looked down at her hands, which were no longer trembling or marked by past bruises. She felt her body was healing, right down to her innermost core. The physical changes mirrored the emotional ones; gone was the fragile, broken woman who had been under Gary's control for so long. In her place stood a survivor, determined to rebuild her life.

"Lucy, I finally feel like myself again," she confessed, tears welling in her eyes. "I'm no longer trapped in a cage of fear and pain. It's as if I've emerged from a cocoon, transformed."

"Annie, you're stronger than you ever realized," Lucy replied, her voice filled with admiration. "You've not only overcome the horrors of your past but also ensured that others won't suffer the same fate. There is one more trial you need to face with Sebastian".

"I know," said Annie. "This one will be a hard one."

As they walked together down the hallway, Annie's thoughts turned inward. For years, she had been haunted by the memories of Gary's abuse – the endless nights spent cowering in terror, the cruel words that had cut her down, and the heavy hand that had struck her repeatedly. But now she had faced him in a court of law, her voice strong and unwavering as she recounted her ordeal. She had finally risen above her abuser.

Annie took a deep breath, inhaling the scent of polished wood and the faint trace of rain from outside. The oppressive atmosphere of the courtroom seemed to fade away, replaced by an air of hope and rebirth. She fought against Gary's control, reclaiming her life and future. As she passed through the grand entrance of the courthouse and stepped onto the rain-slicked pavement, Annie felt a renewed sense of purpose and determination.

"Whatever comes next," she whispered, "I'm ready."

CHAPTER 10

Annie stood on the rain-soaked balcony of her new penthouse apartment, sipping on a glass of champagne. The city skyline stretched before her, an array of twinkling lights that seemed to go on infinitely. She breathed in the crisp, fresh air, the scent of possibility and freedom filling her lungs. It starkly contrasted with the suffocating atmosphere in her old town, where the weight of secrets had been almost unbearable. But now, she was free.

"Cheers, Gary," she whispered, raising her glass towards the heavens with a wicked grin. The money from her meticulously orchestrated plan – his money – had given her the means for this new life far away from him and Sebastian. With every sip of her bubbly indulgence, she reveled in the fruits of her cunning. Oh, how she had played them both like pawns on a chessboard.

"Annie, are you all right?" asked a concerned neighbor from the floor below, craning her head up from her less luxurious balcony.

"Never better, darling!" Annie replied sweetly, her eyes sparkling with mischief. "Just celebrating new beginnings."

"Good for you," the neighbor smiled, retreating into her apartment with an approving nod.

As Annie took another sip of her champagne, she couldn't help but relive the memories of her previous life. The bruises that had once painted her body like a grotesque canvas were no longer there, yet they still haunted her thoughts. She had been trapped, a caged bird in a gilded prison, her wings clipped by Gary's iron grip. And then there was Sebastian, the man who had promised her salvation, only to become another toxic presence in her life.

But Annie was nothing if not resourceful. She had turned the tables on them both, manipulating their weaknesses to her advantage. She had emerged victorious, leaving behind the darkness that had once threatened to consume her. With each new day, she grew more determined to start over and move on.

"Hello?" a voice from behind her interrupted her thoughts. Annie turned to see the building's concierge, a young man with an eager smile, holding a bouquet of fresh flowers. "These just arrived for you, Miss."

"Thank you," she replied, accepting the flowers with a disarming smile. "You can leave them on the table inside."

As the concierge disappeared back into the elevator, Annie walked back inside her apartment, placing the flowers in a crystal vase on the marble countertop. She admired them for a moment before glancing around her luxurious new space. The city lights flooded in through the floor-to-ceiling windows, illuminating her designer furniture and exquisite artwork – all purchased with

Gary's money. It was a testament to her resourcefulness, a monument to her triumphs.

"Here's to new beginnings," she whispered, raising her glass once more as she stared at the city below. But deep within her twisted mind, Annie knew this wasn't the end. No, it was merely another step in her sinister game. She couldn't escape who she was – not entirely. And somewhere out there, another unsuspecting man would soon ensnare in her web.

But for now, she drank to her victory, savoring the sweet taste of revenge that danced on her lips.

Olivia stepped out of her unmarked police car, raindrops splattering against her face as she squinted at the looming gray clouds. She pulled her coat tighter around her and walked towards the dilapidated house that belonged to Sebastian. Her polished leather shoes clicked on the sidewalk, and she could feel dampness seeping through the soles as she navigated puddles.

"Detective Anderson," greeted Officer Wilson, who had been guarding the crime scene, his once-crisp uniform now damp and disheveled from the relentless downpour.

"Officer Wilson," Olivia nodded in acknowledgment. "Why did you call me here? We finished with this investigation. Sebastian is awaiting the court. Did you find anything interesting?"

"Actually, yes," he replied, holding a small evidence bag. Inside was a crumpled piece of paper. "Found it tucked between two floorboards in the living room."

Olivia furrowed her brow as she accepted the bag, carefully unfolding the note. The ink had started to bleed with moisture, but she could still make out the words: "Rescue me - 100K is yours." The handwriting sent a chill down her spine; she recognized it instantly as Annie's.

"Annie wrote this," she murmured, her heart racing as the implications sank in. "She was involved in her own kidnapping."

"Are you sure, Detective?" asked Wilson, concern etched across his face. "Why would she do that?"

"Power, control, revenge," Olivia muttered, more to herself than Wilson. "There's more to Annie than meets the eye. I need to know how long this has been going on. The previous note was printed. This is her handwriting. Why did she change that?"

Determined, she strode back to her car and grabbed a file from the passenger seat. Flipping through the pages, she found what she was looking for a record of incoming mail addressed to Sebastian before he moved to town. Her eyes widened as she spotted the same handwriting on an envelope dated several months prior.

"Annie contacted Sebastian before he even arrived," Olivia whispered, her pulse quickening. "This has been in the works for a long time."

She looked back at Sebastian's house, its dark windows staring back at her like hollow eyes, and shuddered. The rain continued to fall around her, drenching the landscape and casting an eerie pallor on the scene. As much as she wanted to believe that Annie was simply a victim of circumstance, the mounting evidence pointed towards something far more sinister – a complex web of deceit and manipulation that stretched back further than anyone could have anticipated.

The wind picked up, tearing through the trees and shattering Olivia's spine. She knew that unraveling this mystery would be a treacherous path, fraught with twists and turns that would challenge her every step of the way. But she couldn't turn back now. Annie's twisted motivations had ensnared not only Gary and Sebastian but also Olivia herself. And she was determined to see it through, whatever the cost.

"Officer Wilson," she called out, steeling herself against the biting cold. "Let's gather everything we can from Sebastian's place. There's still so much more to uncover."

As they started turning the place upside down again. Olivia couldn't shake the feeling that they were only scratching the surface of a dark, dangerous game that showed no signs of ending anytime soon.

"Detective," Officer Wilson knocked on the half-open window, his voice muffled by the wind and rain. "I found something more, and you need to see this."

"Lead the way, officer," Olivia said, her eyes narrowing with determination as she stepped out into the stormy night.

Officer Wilson guided Olivia to a small room at the back inside the dimly lit house. The walls were lined with fresh wallpaper that started pealing in the corner.

"What's that?" asked Olivia.

"You need to look under this paper, Detective, said Wilson." She pulled the paper out from the corner, and the whole wall of the hardened wallpaper pealed like the orange skin, revealing an array of maps, photographs, and letters – each bearing Annie's handwriting.

"Looks like they've been planning this for months," murmured Olivia, her fingers brushing against a map with several possible escape routes. "But what went wrong? Why didn't they follow through?"

"Maybe she didn't realize that Sebastian wasn't what she thought he was?" suggested Wilson, his expression troubled. "Or perhaps they realized they'd bitten off more than they could chew. Or maybe Sebastian had different agenda, and Annie was played?"

"Either way, we need to find her. Do you know where she moved? It looks like we've all been played." Olivia replied, her voice heavy with concern.

As Olivia studied the evidence scattered before her, she couldn't help but feel a sense of admiration for Annie. Beneath her gentle exterior lay a cunning mind capable of orchestrating such an elaborate scheme. Yet, as she traced the path of Annie's twisted deception, she felt a growing unease. What kind of person could plot such a devious trap – one designed to ensnare her abusive husband, Gary, and the enigmatic Sebastian?

"Officer Wilson, what do you make of this?" Olivia asked, gesturing to a series of coded messages. "Seems like Annie was giving Sebastian specific instructions."

"Could be he was just a pawn in her game," Wilson suggested hesitantly.

"Maybe," Olivia conceded, her mind turning over the possibilities like a Rubik's cube. "Or maybe he was more than that."

As Olivia continued to delve deeper into the evidence, the full extent of Annie's twisted intentions became clear. She had orchestrated her kidnapping with Sebastian, but something had gone sideways. Now, with Gary and Sebastian both ensnared in her web, she was free to pursue her next sinister plan – one that involved another unsuspecting man.

"Her next target," Olivia whispered, her voice tinged with dread and admiration. "We have to stop her, Wilson. Before it's too late."

"Agreed," he said grimly, his gaze meeting hers with a steely resolve. "Let's bring her to justice."

The city's skyline stretched out before Annie, a vast tapestry of glass and steel that shimmered like an urban mirage under the relentless sun. She stood on the rooftop of a high-rise, her eyes fixed on the teeming streets below as she contemplated her newfound freedom.

"Annie!" a voice called out from behind her. It was a gorgeous woman. Her long black hair cascaded down her shoulders, and her face shows of concern as she approached her.

"Amara," she said, barely glancing at her. "I thought you were still in hiding."

"Couldn't stay away any longer," she replied, stepping towards her. "I had to see how everything played out."

"Played out?" Annie echoed, her voice dripping with disdain. "You mean after Sebastian kidnapped me, and I had to improvise?"

"Everything worked out in the end, didn't it?" Amara asked defensively, her hands fidgeting at her sides. "Gary and Sebastian are behind bars, just like you wanted."

"True," she conceded, returning to the sprawling metropolis beneath them. "But now there's another man out there, waiting to be ensnared in my web."

Amara frowned. "What do you mean? You're not planning to do this again, are you?"

"Of course," she replied coolly. "I've only just begun, my love. There are so many more who need to be taught a lesson."

The wind whipped around them, its icy tendrils cutting through the air like razor blades. Despite the bitter chill, the fire in Annie's eyes remained undimmed, her determination unwavering. She could feel the weight of Amara's stare as she tried to make sense of her actions, but she refused to be swayed by her confusion.

"Annie, listen to me," she implored, her voice strained with desperation. "We can't keep doing this. You've made your point and shown everyone that you're no longer a victim. Isn't that enough?"

"Enough?" she scoffed, the word dripping from her lips like venom. "You think I went through all this just to prove a point? No, Amara. This is about justice."

"Justice?" Amara echoed, her confusion giving way to disbelief.

"Annie, what we did – it's not right. We can't keep hurting people like this."

"Justice isn't always pretty, Amara," she replied, her voice laced with steel. "And neither am I."

As she spoke, a cacophony of sirens wailed in the distance, their shrill cries punctuating the tense silence between them. The sound sent a shiver down Amara's spine, but Annie remained unfazed, her gaze never leaving the cityscape before her.

"Time's running out for us," Amara said, her voice barely audible over the din of the sirens. "They'll catch up to us eventually. Don't you see that?"

"Let them try," she whispered, her eyes narrowing as she focused on a lone figure walking along the sidewalk below. Her next target, perhaps?

"Annie, please," Amara pleaded one last time, her voice cracking under the strain. "Let's just walk away from all this. We can start over somewhere else. You've been hurt enough. I can't constantly worry about you."

"Start over?" she mused, a cruel smile playing at the corners of her lips. "Oh, don't worry, Amara. I intend to do just that."

With those chilling words, she turned and disappeared into the shadows of the rooftop, leaving Amara standing alone in the cold, her heart heavy with dread and uncertainty.

"Annie!" Amara called out, her voice barely carrying over the sound of raindrops striking the pavement. "Annie, wait! I'm coming with you."

The End

Or is it?